# By Salt Water

## *Acknowledgements*

Some of these stories have appeared in the following publications, sometimes in slightly different form: 'Pinkeens', and 'Secret Passages' in *The Irish Press*; 'Charm' and 'Majella's Quilt' in *Descant*; 'Deep Down' in *The Irish Times*, *North Dakota Quarterly* and *Virgins and Hyacinths* (Attic Press 1993); 'Blue Murder' in *Stet*; 'Nesting' in *Krino;* 'Camouflage' in *Force 10*; 'Dreams of Sailing' in *The Sunday Tribune*; and 'Ohio by the Ocean' in *Crab Orchard Review*.

The author wishes to thank the Tyrone Guthrie Centre, Annaghmakerrig, for space, quiet and good food.

# BY SALT WATER

stories by Angela Bourke

NEW
ISLAND
BOOKS

**By Salt Water**
*Stories by Angela Bourke*
is first published in 1996
in Ireland by
**New Island Books,**
2 Brookside,
Dundrum Road,
Dublin 14,
Ireland.

ISBN 1 874597 39 1

New Island Books receives financial assistance from
**The Arts Council (An Chomhairle Ealaíon),**
Dublin, Ireland.

Cover design by Jon Berkeley
from an etching by Gráinne Dowling
Typeset by Graphic Resources
Printed in Ireland by Colour Books, Ltd.

*For the friends and family who have kept me afloat.*

# CONTENTS

# DEEP DOWN

I told Liam a story last night. His hand was on my stomach
under my dress and I thought it might make him stop. It wasn't
that I didn't like it. His hand was huge. I couldn't get over the
size of it, but it was warm. The eyes were the same as I
remembered. Brown eyes that kept on looking at me after I
thought he'd look away, so I started to tell him about this thing
that happened hundreds of years ago, a story I often think
about since I heard it. It's in a manuscript, but it happened not
far from my own home—a place called Clonmacnois, on the
Shannon. A lot of medieval things happened there.

It was in a church, with a whole crowd of people and a
priest saying Mass, just after the Consecration, and the people
heard a terrible racket, like something dragging along the
roof. They all ran out and looked up, and there was a boat up
there in the sky. An ordinary boat, like you'd see on the sea,
or on a lake, but it was up above the roof of the church, just
hanging in the sky. They were looking at the bottom of it. The
light is very clear in Clonmacnois, especially when the river
floods.

The anchor was caught in the church door. It was on the end of a long rope coming down through the air, and it was caught in the door they had just come out through. That's what the noise was.

There must have been a terrible commotion. You can imagine them all standing around in the cold with their red faces looking up, but the next thing was a man with no clothes on, just some kind of cloth, swimming down towards them from the boat to get the anchor loose. I have to hold my breath just thinking about it. I'd have been scared stiff.

Some of the men grabbed him and held on to him. He was fighting to get away, but then they had to let him go. He said "You're drowning me," and they could see they were, so they stood back and he flew up away from them.

His own people dragged him into the boat up above, and off they went, away across the sky the way they'd come.

I often wonder if any ancestors of mine were there. They all went back into the church, and the priest finished Mass. They always have to, I believe. It must have been hard for them, coming out at the end, not knowing if the world was changed, or only them.


Liam gave me his jacket getting out of the car because the wind was chilly after the dancehall. It came down to my knees, but it kept me warm. I never knew a leather jacket was so heavy. He made me take off my shoes as well, so I wouldn't ruin them on the beach. But what in the name of God was I doing there? What possessed me?

I'd no idea who he was at the beginning. I don't think I did. Anyone would have noticed him, the way he danced—like a ballet dancer. He reminded me of *West Side Story*, in the tight jeans and the leather jacket—or your man Baryshnikov, the way the hair was flopping onto his forehead. He was taller than the rest of them as well. Longer legs.

A lot of the men around here are good dancers, but they're more heavy-set—their centre of gravity is more in the seat of their trousers. I like dancing with them. I love it when they swing me off the ground and I just go with it, so my feet don't miss a beat when I hit the floor again. I like their strong wrists and the way they laugh a lot. But I don't think I'd ever lust after them, if you know what I mean.

I remembered some of them last night, from when I used to come and stay with Gracie. Men I used to think were old are only five or six years older than me—but then I was only about nineteen. They haven't changed much. Not compared with the women. I got a real shock when I saw some of them—girls that used to be beautiful. Now they're fat and half their teeth are gone and their hair is grey.

It always did me good to come here, I'm ashamed to say. I don't mean the sea air. That'd do anyone good, and all the walking—but the dances, and people fancying me. A suitcase of clean clothes and my hair washed, and off I'd go. I thought I was so glamorous.

Of course at home there were never that many people around. The farms are bigger. I used to feel like an awkward big lump beside the town girls—half asleep and nothing to say, the way you'd see a caterpillar chewing its way through a cabbage leaf. But then I'd come down here and I'd turn into a butterfly, and that's what I was looking for this time too, in spite of what I told Eamonn. I was starting to feel like a fat green lump again. That's not a good sign when you're walking around with fifteen-hundred pounds' worth of diamond engagement ring on your finger.

I didn't say anything to Liam about Eamonn. The ring is back at home where I left it, in the drawer with my Irish dancing medals, and the subject never came up. He didn't even ask me where I was living now. It would have sounded foolish, at that hour of the night. There was so much noise in the hall anyway. Nobody was talking. It's the old-fashioned sort of place. The men all stay on one side and the women are all along the other. They have to walk across the floor to ask you to dance, and there's no such thing as saying no either, unless the man is really footless. When Liam came along he just reached in between two other girls and took hold of my hand, and I just followed him.

His hand was warm, holding on to mine between sets. Dry. He was smiling over my head at the band, but he didn't say anything for ages.

I said nothing either, and now I wonder am I mad? I hardly said a word all evening, to tell the truth, until that time we got back into the car, but that's no excuse.

He did all the talking.

Such a memory! But I should have known better. God almighty—is he even twenty-one?

"Are you Linda Reilly?" he asked me at the end of the third set.

You could have knocked me down.

"Yes," I said. But how did he know? He was young and gorgeous, towering over me, holding onto my hand. You'd think he had to look after me.

"You used to be my babysitter." His teeth were perfect too.

"Oh my God!" It was like opening one of those dolls and finding another one inside. I knew what it was. "Don't tell me. You're not one of the Dunnes?"

"Liam," he said, grinning all over his face, "I knew you the minute I saw you. You came to stay with Gracie Ryan. You minded us when our mother went to hospital."

I used to take them to the beach. Or they used to take me. The same beach we were on last night. Three of them. Liam was the eldest. All the Dunnes were blond, but he was the only one with brown eyes. He used to follow me around. He'd stay sitting with me when the other two were off having adventures. I thought he was worried about his mother.

"I used to dream about you," he said with his arm around me, sitting on the same big rock, after he kissed me the first time. "Did you know that? I was only nine, but I used to go to sleep all excited, thinking about my lovely babysitter."

That smile again. Nobody around here has teeth that good. I could even see them in the dark.

"I couldn't believe it when I walked in there tonight and saw you. You haven't changed a bit, you know."

I nearly choked when he said that, looking at the size of him.

"You have," I said, and we laughed ourselves silly at that. The rock was cold under us, but the sky was warm. And we had his jacket.

All the things you hear about strange men.

Babysitting is different. If kids like you, you feel all strong looking after them. And the funny thing is you feel safe—even after they grow up over six feet and hold your face in their two hands with their two thumbs on the edges of your mouth and their tongue kissing deep into it.

The only thing I worried about was corrupting him, and that made me laugh all over again as soon as I thought of it. I wasn't teaching Liam Dunne anything he didn't know already.

He was the one that started it. He was the one who said it was too cold for me, we should go back to the car.

Something stopped me all the same, in the car. I wasn't cold any more and with his hand on my stomach my whole body felt like some creamy liquid you could pour out of a jug, but then someone's headlights went across the sky. Everyone knows everyone else's car around here. When it's dark you can feel you're the only people for miles, but you never are. Liam's mouth was up against my ear and I could feel his hot whispering, "Trust me," he said, "I'll take care of you. It'll be all right. Just trust me."

I could suddenly see myself in front of a whole crowd of people, holding onto the jug with the last drops dripping out. I was already feeling the relief of warm skin after all the harshness of denim and zips, but I made him stop.

"My mother would love to see you again," Liam said. Maybe that was it. He was sure she'd be delighted, but I could imagine the long cold look she'd give me, the questions about what I'm doing now, am I married yet? Oh, engaged? And what does he do? And where's your ring? Another long hard look, with Liam looking hurt and young, his face up near the low ceiling, not understanding.

I opened the window on my side to let the sound of the waves in. The wind came clean and salty, cooling our skin. That was when I told him about the boat in Clonmacnois.

"I was never there," he said, tucking his shirt in, "but I heard about it. All the monks. It was a big city, I believe."

"Was it?" I said, "I didn't know that."

"And you living beside it?" He sat back in his seat and took a packet of sweets out of somewhere, the way Eamonn would reach for his cigarettes.

"We had a teacher at the Tech that told us about it. I used to love all them stories. I never heard that one before though."

"Could we go now, do you think?" I asked him. It was nearly three in the morning. He turned the key to start the engine, and I wound up my window.

"You mightn't believe what I'm going to tell you," he said, coming up over the rise past the first houses. His voice was grim, "but something like that happened my grandfather back out there."

"Out where?"

"In the bay there, a bit off the Head."

I sucked on my sweet. He must eat them all the time. They tasted like his kisses.

"He was out with three other fellows, fishing for cod. They're all dead now. The last of them went Christmas last year."

I waited, looking at the small haystacks and the fuchsia hedges appearing and disappearing in front of us when the headlights hit them.

"One of the other fellows was at the helm, and my granda had a line out. He felt a heavy sort of weight, and when he pulled it in, what do you think was on it?"

"What?"

"A baby."

I felt an awful lurching. The sweet was in my mouth, but I didn't know what it was doing there. Why was he telling me this? And on a line. Hooked. A baby on a hook—not even in a net.

When I was about fifteen someone buried a dead baby in the corner of a field near us. Nobody let on they knew anything about it. The guards came around all the houses, but the girl was already gone to England.

I opened the window and Liam looked around at me. "It wasn't dead," he said quickly. He put his hand on my knee. Warm again. "That's what I'm telling you. It was a live baby, fit and well, with clothes on it."

"How could it be alive?" I laughed with the relief.

"That's what I don't know. All I know is my grandfather was one of the best fishermen around here, and he wasn't making it up."

"They don't fish here any more, do they?"

"Not since 1968."

"Is that when the drownings were?"

"Two boat-loads of men in one night. My granda was one of them."

Liam was stopping the car. My guesthouse was in on our left, but I wanted to hear more.

"I didn't know that. You must have only been a baby then."

He turned off the engine, then the lights.

"I wasn't even born. My mother was carrying me. I have all his things above in the house. She kept them for me. I'm called after him."

"Did she tell you the story too?"

"She did. And she made me promise I'd never go fishing for a living."

"It's a dangerous life all right."

"There was another bit to the story too," he said slowly, "only it wasn't from my mother I heard it."

"What was that?" I felt like his babysitter again. Careful. Maybe it was the houses around, or the paved road.

"One of the other old fellows that was out that day used to say they had to throw the child back."

"Back into the water?" Funny I never even asked him what they did with it.

The car was very quiet with the engine off. I could see Liam's face in the light from the sky. He was looking straight ahead, leaning on the steering wheel, not touching me.

"I don't know," he said quickly, "but that's what they did. He said a woman came up beside the boat in the water and cursed them up and down for hooking the child out of its cradle down below."

I didn't laugh. He wasn't laughing. I saw his hand go to the key and come back. His mother was on her own in the house, I suppose. He'd told me his two brothers were in Boston, and I knew his father was dead years ago. She'd probably lie awake till she heard the car.

"I'll go in," I said. "Thanks for the lift."

He started the engine. The lights flashed a screen of stone wall and fuchsia hedge up in front of us.

"Sure I might see you tomorrow." A bit of a smile at last.

"Sure you might, I suppose," I said, smiling back. This was the usual chat, visitors flirting with locals. Harmless really.

I walked up to the front door, but I didn't go in. I stood there on my own in the quiet night, watching the car's headlights cut through the dark sky until I couldn't see them any more.

# THE WHALE IN THE GARDEN

We were looking into a rock pool on the beach when Miss Montague came down past the grotto, where the statue of Our Lady is. Liam Shea and Tom Shea were down on their hunkers poking at a thing in the water, and I was standing with my big sister, looking. When I saw her I pulled Helena's dress to warn her. Tom had the stick, poking a tight red shiny thing stuck to the rock.

"That's the rock's arsehole. See? Do you not believe me?" He was staring at Helena, trying to make her go red. Helena was trying to see, but she looked up when I pulled her dress. When Tom Shea noticed he started to go red himself. He looked around very slowly.

Miss Montague said "Hello children." She nodded at all of us, smiling, and Tom and Liam stood up.

"Oh," she said. Tom and Liam moved over to let her in. "It's a sea-anemone. Leave it alone and watch. It's like a flower you know, even though it eats things."

We all stood around the pool, watching, and the red blob on the rock opened up. Little starry fingers unfolded from the middle and waved gently in the water.

"That's how it gets its food—it moves those tentacles in the water till it catches some tiny creature swimming by, then it puts it in its mouth."

The thing on the rock folded itself back into a red blob while she was still talking.

"I don't see any mouth," I said.

Helena whispered, "Sssh!" but Miss Montague heard me.

"Its mouth is in the middle," she said, smiling down, "along with its stomach. It's a funny place to have a mouth, isn't it? Now it's digesting its food, you see? I'm glad you're looking into these little rock pools. The sea is full of life, you know. Every one of these pools is a little community." She smiled again, and then she walked away.

In the winter it was too dark to play when we got home from school, so we never went to the beach. Then the days got longer and the wind was dry again. Our mothers hung out long lines of washing, and everybody's father except ours hauled seaweed up from the beach in cartloads to put on the fields. They spread it in beautiful even stripes on the grass so they could dig in between them and make beds for the potatoes to grow.

It didn't get dark in the evening till after our tea. Whenever we saw Miss Montague I used to wave to her and she waved back. Helena said I was a show-off.

After the big spring tide there were new things on the beach. The whale was one of them, on the stony part near the old harbour, and I found it first. It was gigantic, lying on the stones, but when Liam and Tom Shea came, they said it wasn't big enough to be a whale.

"Sure a whale'd be as big as a trawler!" Tom said. "This yoke's only about as big as a rowing boat." He pushed the side of its body with his wellington and left a sandy mark.

Whatever it was, its nose was long and pointy, it had big scabby blotches all over it, but no bits were missing.

"It probably swam up here by itself, and then it couldn't get back to the sea so it died," Tom said. "It's going to give off a right stink, whatever it is. They'll have to tow it away out where the tide can take it."

"They will not!" I said to him, all snooty, but I was worried. I couldn't bear them to send it back after it came all the way to our beach from far away, as if we weren't even interested.

Helena said she was going to tell our father about it, and he'd know what to do, because he was a teacher. All the way home I was arguing with her. He never let us keep dead things, but she just said I was stupid.

"It's not your whale anyway," I said. I hated when she made me cry. "It's *mine*. I found it first."

We were passing the gate of Rose Cottage and Helena was laughing. "See how much you like your stupid old whale when it starts to get smelly, cry-baby! Anyway I bet it isn't a whale."

Miss Montague had smooth green grass behind her gate, and a white seat. Her house was the only one with a name. When I saw her in the garden I stopped.

"What are you *doing*?" Helena shouted at me in a whisper. "Come *on*!" But Miss Montague was waving, and Helena couldn't do anything, because she was coming over to talk to us.

"What's the matter, Maeve?" she asked me. I didn't know she knew my name. I didn't know what to say.

"She's crying because there's a dead fish on the beach and she thinks it's a whale," Helena said.

"Oh dear! What kind of fish? Is it very big?"

"Not that big," Helena said, but I said "It is. It's huge. It's bigger than the seat", and Miss Montague turned around to look at the white seat behind her.

"Well," she said, "that's certainly a big fish. I'd like to see it. You'd better run along home now, but maybe tomorrow if it's still there, you could show it to me? I have a book that might tell us what it's called."

"So nyah!" I said to Helena.

"A whale isn't a fish at all, as far as I know," our father said, and Helena laughed, but Miss Montague said the same thing the next day.

"Your father's right. Whales are mammals, the same as us. They have warm blood, and they breathe air."

She showed us a picture in her book, of a whale blowing a huge fountain out of the water.

"They sing to each other too," she said. "Did you know that?"

I shook my head. I could see Helena didn't believe her, but our father had said we were to be good when we showed Miss Montague the whale, and listen carefully to what she said. "There's no one like the Protestants for nature study," he said, "but that lady knows more about it than most of them."

"I think this is definitely a whale," Miss Montague said. It was lying on its side on the beach with its eyes closed. Liam and Tom were guarding it.

"How do you know it's not a shark?" Helena asked. She was starting to get interested.

"A shark is a fish. Look at the tail."

We all looked.

"That tail would flap up and down in the water, wouldn't it?"

We looked at the big flappy tail and then back up at her. "But a fish's tail doesn't go up and down," she moved her hand up and down, "it goes from side to side," and her hand waved over and back in the air.

All the whales in her book had the same kind of tail that was flat on the ground if they were lying on their stomach. They looked friendlier than sharks, but the pictures were of when they were alive. Miss Montague walked right up around the front of our whale and knelt down to put her hand on its chest.

"I think it's a female." She looked up at us, "Whales are mammals, you know. They suckle their young."

I saw the Sheas sniggering behind her back, she said it so loud. Helena got red, but I don't think I did.

"And if I'm not mistaken," Miss Montague said, "this is one of the beaked whales," and she sat down on a rock to draw a picture of it.

"I think some friends of mine in Dublin will be very interested in this, but we'll have to do something soon. It's getting a bit sniffy, isn't it?"

Even Liam and Tom smiled back at her this time. The way she climbed around the whale with her measuring tape, you could see she really liked it.

"Maeve," Miss Montague called the next day, "Helena." We were walking back to school after our dinner. "I rang up my friend in Dublin and he's very excited about your whale. He wants it for the museum, but I'm afraid there's a problem."

We stopped at her gate. Our father went past on his bike, but I didn't care if we were late.

"He said it sounds like quite a rare whale, but they're short of staff at the museum and they can't possibly send anyone down this week."

"Tom and Liam's daddy is going to tow it out behind his boat tomorrow," I said. "Then it'll be gone."

"I know, Maeve. They can't leave it rotting on the beach. But I have another idea. I think we should bury it."

Then she told us what she wanted. She said if a few men would come with a cart, and some ropes, they could bring it up to her garden, behind Rose Cottage. "John-Joe Neill is already digging a hole in there for it, but he'd be glad if anyone would help him. I'm going to see a few people this afternoon. Maybe you could ask your father what he thinks as well?"

We went to her house after school to tell her our father said yes. She brought us out to the kitchen and gave us cold tea brack with butter on it, and milk. Then she explained about burying the whale.

"It would be a great loss if we couldn't manage to save the skeleton," she looked across the table at us as though we were grown up. "And the best way to do it is to let the worms do the work."

If we buried it in the ground for a few years the bones would come up nice and clean and scientists could put them back together and learn things from them. And the museum would put a notice beside the skeleton saying it was found in Trananewrogue.

At the back of Rose Cottage when we went to look, behind a high wall, trees were growing, like trees in pictures. Usually trees in Trananewrogue looked like somebody's hair that was standing beside the sea, with the wind blowing it. The wind from the Atlantic was so strong and salty it made them grow humpy and sideways, but Miss Montague's garden was sheltered, and behind the wall was warmer and quieter than outside. She showed us things called loganberries along the wall. They looked shabby and withered, but Miss Montague said they'd be like raspberries when they grew, only bigger. She said we could come back in the summer and taste them.

In the corner just inside the big wooden gates was the hole for the whale, with John-Joe still digging it, and some big boys from our school already helping him. Then we heard Liam and Tom outside with their big brother, coming to cut off the old rusty padlock and oil the hinges. Helena just got out of the way in time. The gates swung open and a big square of light came into the garden. We could see all the way out the bog road, with the mountains behind.

Before we went home, Miss Montague brought us in to meet her father, sitting with white hair in a big armchair. He used to be in charge of the Protestant church in Grange, but now there were no Protestants left, and Canon Montague had had a stroke anyway, so he couldn't be a minister any more. He sat in the dining room at the back of their house all day, with his stick beside his chair, looking out at the garden.

"Father's very interested in Natural History," Miss Montague said. The Canon made little noises and smiled on one side of his face.

"You should come again whenever you like," she said. "This house used to have lots of visitors."

After tea we went back to Rose Cottage, me on the crossbar of our father's bike and Helena on the carrier. The whale came up the bog road on the seaweed cart, with men walking behind it and dogs running around barking at the smell. People were standing with torches, and about twelve men were filling in the hole. We stood watching until it was nearly pitch dark and then our father said we had to go, even though they weren't finished. Lots of boys were still there, and we could hear people talking, but we couldn't see them, only their cigarettes.

When we said goodnight to Miss Montague she said again we should come anytime and visit. We could just come in, because there was no lock on the big gates any more.

She was glad of the company, she said. It gave her an excuse to bake. We helped her in the garden too. New leaves came on the loganberries, and then lovely big red fruit, and we helped to plant the asparagus. It was in the corner inside the gates, on top of the whale, not with the other vegetables. You have to wait a very long time before you can eat asparagus, Miss Montague said, but it's worth it, because it's more delicious than any other vegetable. It would give the worms a chance to get on with their work. There'd be no digging near the whale till it was all gone except clean bones.

Helena went to boarding school in September, but I still kept going to Miss Montague's on my own. We worked in the garden, and when she was making her Christmas cake and her puddings she let me help.

"I always used to help my mother with her Christmas baking," she said. "I used to take my turn doing all the mixing."

I never thought of Miss Montague being a little girl before. I waited for her to say something else, but she kept looking down.

"I never thought she'd die," she said suddenly. Then she let her breath out hard and smiled at me, "I've been lucky really. I don't think there's anywhere in the world more beautiful than Trananewrogue."

I could hear the clock ticking, but all Miss Montague said was: "Make sure you get your education, Maeve. It's very valuable."

I got into the habit of waving to the Canon, sitting in the dining-room window. Then one day in the garden, we were digging up beds after the frost, and he wasn't there when I looked.

Miss Montague seemed very tired that day. She said he was going to die soon. She didn't know what would happen then. I wondered about our whale, but I couldn't think how to ask her.

When the Canon did die, the funeral wasn't in our church, on account of him being Protestant, and I didn't see Miss Montague at all. Mammy said she was gone to stay with her cousins in Limerick for a while, and I waited for her to come back.

It was a beautiful summer. The loganberries ripened along the wall in the garden and I picked a lot of them, but there were too many for me. The birds ate them, but some just stayed, turning into red drippy mush. Everything was growing wild. I could see the asparagus, but I didn't know what to do with it. Even John-Joe didn't come to cut the grass, so I could hardly make out where the flowerbeds were.

Helena came home from boarding school but she wasn't interested in the garden, and when I wanted to talk about the whale and the asparagus she wasn't interested in them either. I used to go up to Rose Cottage by myself and think about them. It was hard to believe the whale was really under there.

I was starting boarding school in September, and I was afraid I'd be gone before Miss Montague got back. Then one morning there was a sign out in front, in the long grass: FOR SALE.

I only had a chance to go one more time to the garden, and I stood inside the big gates, looking over at the green feathery asparagus. The sun was shining and it was very quiet. I could imagine the whale swimming happily down there, waving its green frilly wings through the water, singing.

# DREAMS OF SAILING

About three weeks after I met Tony we went out to Howth and climbed up the hill with a bottle of wine, instead of going to our History lecture. Tony made up a prayer to the pagan gods, and before we drank the wine he poured some on the ground. He was going to be a poet. He hardly ever went to lectures. The psychiatrist in college had told him he was desperately sensitive, and he was convinced all the lecturers were fools.

The wine made me dizzy. It was freezing up there, but Tony was in his element.

"*Thalassa*!" he kept saying, "That's the Greek for sea."

He had a big heavy coat on though.

The grass was damp and I was drunk. The sea was grey like the sky, and Tony started to talk about celebrating our love.

"Irish people have no sensuality," he said. "All the rain, and drinking beer all the time. It'd just be sordid if we did it here."

He thought we should wait till we got to the south of France. Under a blue pagan sky, he said. He'd never been out of Ireland and neither had I, but then neither of us had ever been to bed with anyone either.

We were supposed to go to France after the exams. Normandy, then Brittany, then Paris, then on down south for the grape-picking. Tony was going to do the talking—he did French. We were going to get brown and healthy walking along dusty white roads, but then he failed his exams and went home to Waterford. To tell the truth I was relieved—he was starting to get on my nerves.

I went to Goleen instead, to stay with my aunts, and that's where I met Kevin. He was the exact opposite—big and tall and cheerful, zooming all over the place in a white Volkswagen van. His father had a hardware shop in the town and Kevin was all set to take over and expand it as soon as he finished college.

Every time I saw Kevin he was doing something. He loved being out of breath. I don't think he ever read a book. I often wonder if Bridie or Sally noticed anything, or what they thought of it all.

Bridie and Sally are my father's sisters, but they're much older than he is. We were always told they weren't interested in children, so I didn't know them well. I was delighted when they asked me to stay, that they thought I was interesting enough. But when I got to Goleen there wasn't a lot to do, except go for walks along the cliff path. I wandered down the pier a few times, but I felt too self-conscious on my own, not knowing anybody.

Then Bridie said "Why don't you go up to the sailing club? That's where all the young people go in the evenings."

Bridie and Sally took life so calmly. Anything they wanted to do, they just did.

And it was as simple as that. I bought myself a Harp and lime at the bar, and people talked to me. They all asked "What do you sail?" but there was plenty of noise and I didn't mind just standing listening. Then one of the girls said "Oh there's Kevin," and someone called him over.

He started talking to me straight away, "I saw you down the pier yesterday, didn't I?"

Some very brown people with a lot of rings on their fingers stood near us, just back from a cruise to Brittany. They were talking about a boat called the *Sea Serpent*, and someone called Caroline who was staying on in France for a year. I think it was her boat. They kept saying things to Kevin, but he kept coming back to stand beside me, and at the end of the night he offered me a lift.

When we got to the aunts' house he just sat revving the engine. I got out of the van. It wasn't that I thought he fancied me—he was just being polite to a stranger. But he leaned out the window, "I'm trying out a Laser tomorrow afternoon if you want to come."

Whatever a Laser was.

The next day the white van stopped beside me on the road and the door on my side opened.

"Come on. Jump in."

I jumped in. When you've been walking around a place for days it's wonderful to get a lift.

I figured a Laser must be some kind of boat. That was all any of them talked about. Kevin said it was really fast. He was dying to try it. It was light enough to carry on a roof-rack. You could store it anywhere.

I thought of our house, all the bikes in the hall.

It turned out a Laser was like a sailboard, only much wider. White and long and pointed, and for something lightweight it was heavy. We loaded some of it into the van and the rest up onto the roof-rack. I was amazed at all the bits and pieces. I knew about the sail, and the mast, but there was the boom as well, and the rudder, and the tiller, and a thing called a daggerboard — a big canvas bag of things.

At the beach we did the whole operation in reverse. Kevin gave me the narrow end, but I thought I'd collapse carrying it down to the water. He went back up to the van and changed into a wetsuit. He looked hilarious, but I didn't let on. He was dead serious. For someone so cheerful he didn't have much sense of humour.

I sat up in the sand-dunes with my clothes on, reading, and Kevin went over and back, over and back in front of me. Every so often I'd look up and wave. I was reading *The French Lieutenant's Woman*, so I was a bit preoccupied, but I saw him hanging out over the side once, and he capsized a few times. Then I helped him drag the Laser out of the water and we did the whole business again, taking it apart and carrying it back to the van.

Driving back, Kevin looked like a big red baby, with his hair all wet and plastered to his head, but he was delighted with the Laser. He said he was definitely going to buy it, only he called it *she*.

"She's incredible, you know. She's so responsive. She really lets you feel the sea and the wind." He wriggled his shoulders under the flannel shirt, sighing and grinning at the same time, "That old *Sea Serpent* isn't sailing at all."

Something made me hold my breath.

"Is that the boat that went to Brittany? Did you sail on it too?"

"I used to crew on her all the time."

"Why didn't you go on the cruise then?"

"Well," he said, "myself and Caroline broke up before she went away. I thought I'd give it a miss."

Caroline again. I imagined somebody rich and brown. A brilliant sailor. Fluent French.

"Were you and Caroline going together?" Goleen was like a photograph to me—I forgot other people had lives there before this summer.

"What? Oh yeah, for years. Sure we were living together all last year in Dublin."

No wonder he didn't fancy me. I bet he could spot an anxious little virgin a mile away. It made me more irritated than ever about Tony.

"I'm definitely going to buy it," Kevin said again. "I'll tell him tonight. Would you fancy having a go yourself? They can take two, you know. We could probably get hold of a wetsuit for you."

I was so annoyed, I would have said yes to anything.


So there I was the next day, wading out to meet him, with the sea seeping sneakily onto my skin through this huge wetsuit. It belonged to someone called Dave, and he must have been fifteen inches broader across the shoulders than I was. I felt grotesque. Like a Martian.

I had to sit on the side and hold onto a rope. It was the sheet, and that meant I was the crew. Kevin sat in the stern with the tiller, and that made him the helm. All I had to do was sit there and keep hold of the rope. I was to let it out or pull it in so the sail didn't flap, and I was supposed to lean in or out to balance us.

Kevin said he'd say "Ready about," when he was going to turn us around, and then "Lee ho!" I was to duck under the boom when I heard that, and get over to the other side without letting go of my rope. I listened in some kind of reckless despair. I had no idea how I'd got this far, so I was just waiting for the rest of it to happen.

But we started off and there was nothing to it. It was like going downhill on a bike and I began to relax. I grinned happily at Kevin and he grinned back, "We might as well take her out in the bay."

He pushed the tiller over a bit. I pulled the sheet in a bit and we started to go fast, out towards America. I was enjoying myself now, leaning out, getting used to the balance of it.

Then Kevin said "Ready about!" and "Lee ho!" as though there was an admiral listening, instead of just me. The boom started swinging gently towards me and I started to do my stuff, ducking under it. But then it stuck, and I saw the thing called the daggerboard sticking up, stopping it from coming any further. Everything shuddered, and very slowly yet all at once, we were in the water, much lower down than before, wet and getting wetter.

I came blubbering up to the surface and Kevin was on the other side of the boat, laughing. This was something I was supposed to take in my stride. Part of the fun, but I wasn't doing it right. My nose was running and my mouth was full of the sea. I had thick rubber sponge all over my body, along with a life-jacket. I couldn't swim—I was crawling on top of the water like one of those insects. There was nowhere I could go. The Laser was face down in the water and the land was miles away.

Kevin was paddling around over there, turning the upside-down boat into the wind, being efficient. I hung in the water, deciding to trust him. At least he knew about capsizes. I was getting used to the feel of my life-jacket—like an armchair in the water. The people in the clubhouse probably did this all the time.

Kevin managed to do something with his feet. He shouted across to me, and up she came.

The mast and the sail came swinging up against the blue sky, with the sun shining on all the drops of water as they poured off. It looked so beautiful and geometric, very high and white and far away. I was beginning to understand why people love sailing so much, even the falling in, when something crashed down on my head.

It was the mast. The top of the mast. I was miles away from it, but it was long. If I'd been standing on concrete instead of on water it would have split my skull. At first I thought it had. It hurt like anything.

"Kevin!" I yelled, and his red face grinned back at me between the waves, further and further away. I kept expecting to lose consciousness. The thing I had on was a buoyancy aid, not a life-jacket. I'd be floating face down in the water.

"I'm hurt, for Christ's sake! I can't do anything!"

I kept swallowing water, but he finally got the boat up again, and it stayed up. He brought it to where I was and hauled me on. Carefully, we made it back to the beach.

Kevin was smiling again by the time we got there, "That was great, wasn't it?"

I didn't say anything, but it didn't matter.

He dropped me off at my aunts' house, "I'll see you tonight then."

By the time I'd had a bath and washed my hair I felt okay. Bridie and Sally were both out. I was aching all over, but I was dry, and going up to the club in the evening I felt I'd had my initiation.

Kevin seemed to think so too. He stood with his arm around me, talking to a man called Bill who'd just bought an oyster bed. Someone mentioned Caroline and I realised Bill was her father. He looked very young.

When closing time came we walked out to the van together and I got in my side.

Kevin drove by the coast road instead of straight down to the village, and when we came to the lay-by near the cliff path he stopped the van. He said we might as well go for a walk, so of course we did, and of course he put his arms around me and we kissed on the cliff path. We walked back up to the van.

"That was a scream today, wasn't it?" he said. He held me against the side of the van. The nights are very short that time of year. There was still a lot of blue in the sky over his shoulder.

"You know when I saw you down on the pier with your book I thought you were a real snooty intellectual, but you have a lovely pair of tits."

I was glad my face was against his shoulder so he couldn't see it.

The next thing he said was "I want to make love to you." He started kissing me again.

"So this is it, is it?"

I haven't any sisters, but sometimes I imagine one, younger than me and a bit cynical. That was her voice inside my head.

"I never thought it'd happen this soon," I muttered to her. "I have to do it sometime."

She grinned at me and shrugged.

Kevin opened the back of the van. There was a piece of carpet on the floor that hadn't been there that afternoon.

"Come on," he said.

It didn't take very long and it hurt like hell and after it was over he handed me a box of tissues. They weren't there in the afternoon either. At least it was dark in there.

We got back into the front and he drove me home. He didn't say anything, and I thought it was because I was a virgin. I thought he was disgusted or disappointed or something, but he gave me a quick, absent-minded sort of a kiss.

"That was great. You'd better go in. See you tomorrow."


I was there another six days, and every day Kevin picked me up at the harbour. We drove to the beach and I helped him get the Laser off the roof-rack and carry it down to the water. We assembled the mast and the boom, and I held the sail while he fed the mast into the sleeve along the side. Then I'd lie in the sun or sit in the sand-dunes with my book and after a while he'd come back, all dripping and exhilarated, and ask me if I'd seen this or that, and I'd go and help him haul the boat out of the water. Every evening we went to the club and every night Kevin drove me home the long way. We stopped in the lay-by on the cliff road and made love in the back of the van. I couldn't honestly say I enjoyed it, but I learned a lot. It turned out he'd never done it with Caroline, even though they had shared a flat. "We had plenty of sex," he said, a bit grumpy when I asked him. "We just never made love."

I nearly laughed, but he was serious, "Caroline wants to keep her virginity till she gets married," he said. "I respect that."

He didn't seem to care if I just lay there, so I was able to think about the whole business. I thought about Tony, with his poetry and his bottles of wine, and Kevin with his heaving and grunting. I thought of all the kinds of people there must be in between, and how I'd like to do it if I got a chance. Maybe I would get a chance now the hard part was over.

I got a lot of reading done in those six days. I finished *The French Lieutenant's Woman* and went on to three or four Jane Austens that were in Bridie and Sally's. I didn't fancy another attempt at sailing. Kevin was still all excited about the Laser, but it was really only made for one person.

# CAMOUFLAGE

The bus had to go slowly up the hill at Slane. It's steep there, coming up from the bridge, and there was ice. On the low granite wall at the Castle gates I saw two cock pheasants, looking heraldic. I nudged Dermot. Two thick coat sleeves, two woolly sweater sleeves, two shirt sleeves away, his elbow was there beside mine. I knew it well, white-skinned and pointed, with fine dark hair above and below. He has very skinny arms, Dermot, but all I could feel was the bulk of sleeves.

"What?" he said.

"Look," I pointed at the pheasants, red and gold, regal, posing together. "They have an aristocratic look about them, haven't they? They go well with the stone." It was the first thing I'd said since Dublin, apart from careful remarks about my cold feet and the smell of diesel and thank God we're moving at last anyway. I was glad of the pheasants, for something safe to talk about. Dermot's interested in wildlife. Every other time I was about to say something I swallowed it instead. I know that road so well, going up and down to Derry, and there were things I wanted to show him, but even passing the flat in Phibsboro, where I lived when I came to Dublin first, I felt the little spring in my throat of wanting to tell him, and then I remembered last night, and the things he'd said.

"What do you mean, aristocratic?" he said now. The bus was going through the village. "Do you mean like useless parasites, no damn good for anything?"

"Pheasants aren't parasites," I tried to laugh. "I just meant they looked as if they belonged there. I thought they looked nice."

"It depends what you mean by parasites," he said, and there was a little bitter silence that made my heart sink again.

"What do you mean? Sure pheasants don't do any harm, do they? You can eat them, after all." I was trying to steer down the middle of whatever was going on.

"Did *you* ever eat one?"

"No," I said.

"Why not?"

"I don't know. I just never did."

"I'll tell you why you never did. Because they're reserved for the rich, that's why. Do you know where those ones came from? Do you know why you suddenly see a whole lot of them this time of the year? I suppose you thought they were wild?"

I nodded, surprised.

"Well they're not wild. They're about the stupidest creatures on this earth and they're hand-reared like chickens in the back yards of stately homes."

"But why?"

"So rich eejits can go out with rifles on their day off and shoot them and think they're the landed gentry, and the landed gentry can live in the style they're accustomed to, that's why. Chinless wonders in navy jumpers and green wellies. You wouldn't catch them keeping chickens, but they'll rear pheasants all right. They haven't a bean—most of them haven't a brain in their head—but they have the right accent, haven't they, and they have the stately home, even if it's falling down around them, so they can charge what they like to the poor buckeejit of a stockbroker for a day's shooting. Don't talk to me about pheasants! Make me sick!"

He sat back in his seat, and I felt the tension go out of him. A woman across the aisle in front of us looked around. I looked out the window. Stupid bitch, why wouldn't she mind her own business? Dermot gets angry a lot, but it doesn't usually bother me. I just breathe quietly in and out, holding still, waiting for it to pass me by, but that wasn't working any more. This time he was like an icy wind, and I was someone standing helplessly at a bus-stop with no coat. It was because of last night, the way he suddenly attacked me: "All you ever talk about is your bloody family and your bloody friends and every goddamn thing they ever did! How can you be so fucking complacent? Do you never *think* about anything?" It was such a shock to me. Of course I think about things. What does he think I'm doing all the time when he's going on and on about his political analysis and his strategies? He did take it all back though, later. Said he was just tired. I was afraid he was going to call the trip off, tell me he wouldn't come after all. I knew he'd like my family when he met them. I just didn't want everything spoiled.

He never said anything about his own family. He didn't talk much about friends either, but he said he loved me. He said we were twins. We used to laugh all the time together, like little kids. When we got dressed in the frosty fog this morning to go for the bus, even after the awful night, we put on two pairs of jeans that belonged to both of us, two soft flannelly shirts he'd bought in London, two big greeny-brown sweaters that I'd knitted, woolly socks we'd bought together in the Scout shop. My brown shoulder-bag was in the rack above my head, and his was on the ground between his feet. We'd bought them together too, and I knew they had exactly the same kind of stuff in them. Only our shoes and our knickers were our own. We used to laugh about being the same size and wearing the same clothes. It didn't even matter whose place we slept in, we could both wear whatever was there. It was usually his place though—freezing, with lino on the floor—and I had a toothbrush there, and a bag of underwear.

I wouldn't be home for Christmas. My mother was disappointed, but what could I do? I was going up now, with presents for everyone, and I was bringing Dermot. Some of what I wanted to say to him was Thank You. Thank you for finding the time. Thank you for coming at last to meet my family. Thank you for letting me show you Derry. We can walk around the Walls, and I'll show you the Bogside and the Creggan. We can go out the Culmore Road, and maybe even up to Grianán. I can't believe it, you know, with all your talk. I can't believe you've never been up North.

On up through the hilly country before Ardee there was fog in the hollow places—white horses' tails in wisps across the road, going on journeys of their own. Above, the sky was clear pale frosty blue. Everything I could see was beautiful in a weird, wintry, albino way. All the green movement of the grass and leaves and branches locked into silent white crystals. I caught my breath to point it out to Dermot, but let it go again. His eyes were closed.

The bus stopped suddenly. A woman with long blonde hair stepped out into the crispy white grass and stood vomiting, holding her hair twisted round her left hand. Dermot opened his eyes and I looked over at him. It's awful to be sick on the bus. I thought our eyes would meet in gratitude that we weren't sick, and we weren't on our own, but he looked away again.

We stopped in Monaghan. The blonde woman was washing her face when I went into the toilets. She asked me if I had a tissue, because the toilet paper was the hard shiny kind. She was like a ghost, so I told her I'd get her a cup of tea when I was getting ours, and she went to sit at a corner table. I followed her with the tray, but Dermot didn't come. He was making a phone call, and his tea just sat looking at us till the bus driver called us.

Back on the bus he still said nothing. I looked out the window and wondered what had got into him lately. He used to be so energetic and cheerful. He used to say people like us were changing the world. He'd sit up all night putting things into envelopes, or he'd arrive in from Limerick and get a phone call, and I'd find a note saying he'd gone to Cork. Sometimes I helped with the envelopes, and I took an awful lot of phone messages. When he was away I usually cleaned up his room. I took loads of stuff to the launderette, and I boiled kettles to wash all the dirty dishes. He was glad I was around. So many women thought of nothing but their looks, he told me. Most of them were so materialistic, they just castrated their men. The country was going to need more women like me. I didn't know about the country, but I was glad to be there when he needed me. He did too much sometimes: too many late nights, too many meetings, and then he'd get these awful cold sores all over his lips. It was like the flu: shivering and aching, and hardly able to walk up the stairs; but he trusted me. I used to put clean sheets on the bed and lie with my arms around him till he fell asleep.

I began to breathe quietly again. If I could just stay calm, he'd get over it, whatever it was. In a field by the road I saw a hare. The way it sat, with its ears pricked up, it looked just like a withered clump of anything. As long as it didn't move, you'd never know it was there. In countries where they have a lot of snow the hares go white in winter, but here they stay brown. I thought again about the pheasants, sitting targets in all their finery. I imagined them flopping up, stupid and clumsy in front of the rifles.

We came to Emyvale, and Dermot was looking past me out the window. That field near the river used to be full of mud and ducks, but I didn't tell him that.

"This is the last town before the border," I said.

I never know exactly how far it is after that. I get nervous. Customs men and soldiers give me the willies. Dermot was sitting up very straight, leaning away from me to look out the front window.

"Are you OK?" I asked him.

He didn't answer. Suddenly, he turned around, and the look on his face was the same as last night. His face was white, but this time he looked more frightened than angry.

"You treat me as if I was a child," he said, "Do you know that? You think I'm just like you, only not as mature, but I'm not. I'm not like you at all." He gathered his coat around him and stood up. "Look," he said, "I'll see you."

The bus slowed down as he pulled himself up the aisle to the driver's seat. It stopped. Dermot got off and then I saw his bag over his shoulder. He stood for a moment with his back to me, his breath clouding into a fog in front of him. The driver leaned over and said something, and I saw Dermot shake his head. I was going to stand up, but the doors swished shut and the bus moved on. The woman across the aisle looked back at me. I looked out the window. I couldn't see Dermot; he must have crossed the road. A mile or so later I was still looking out the window, trying to take it in, when I saw another pheasant. It was a hen this time, brown and ordinary, frumping in the corner of a field with the withered clumps of weed and the cast-off plastic sacks.

At Aughnacloy we bumped carefully forward over the speed ramps, past the checkpoint tower. 5 MPH, the sign said. A soldier's face was behind one tiny window, a camera looked out another. The confidential telephone number was stencilled all along the wall. Report anything suspicious.

A young blond soldier got on the bus, grinning. He wore a baggy uniform, blotched green and brown, nearly the same colour as my sweater. He carried a rifle.

"Wha' a beau' iful day i' is," he said, all glottal stops instead of "t's". He walked down the aisle past my seat, "Come on folks, cheer up!"

# PINKEENS

We used to play hopscotch in the summer. We never played it at school. Probably if you tried in the playground you'd be just standing on one foot, stretching to pick up your piggy and someone playing chasing or catching-hand-chain would charge into you and knock you over. Anyway we wouldn't be allowed to draw on the ground at school. This was in the back lane. We spent nearly all our time out there in the holidays.

We had to go to ten o'clock Mass every morning. After that we could play. The priest at ten o'clock was usually pretty fast, and there was sometimes a wedding or a funeral we could watch, so it wasn't too bad. You didn't have to walk to the church with your mother and father or wear good clothes. The only thing you couldn't do if you were a girl was wear shorts.

That was because of the nuns at school. They said shorts were immodest. If you wore them you made your guardian angel cry and you were an occasion of sin, so anyone that came to school in them got slapped. Every year when we got our holidays the head nun came around all the classes to tell us to go to Mass every morning, and help our mothers, and not to wear immodest clothing. That meant shorts, or short skirts, or any kind of sundress with straps. If we wore them the nuns would find out.

My mother wouldn't have minded. In the photographs in our house of her and her friends up the mountains, nearly all the girls had shorts on. I even had a pair, but I only used to wear them like bathing togs, when we went to the seaside, or on very hot days in the back lane.

The other thing was getting sent out for messages. Somebody's little brother or sister would come out and say "You're wanted," or else your mother would come out to the back gate and call you. Even if it was your turn for hopscotch you had to just go, and if you had shorts on, you had to change into a skirt first.

I never minded going up to the shops, even though I had to come straight back. I'd get a penny or twopence to spend, or I'd see people from school out with their mothers, or maybe doing messages by themselves.

I sometimes saw a whole crowd of boys coming down past the shops together. They were only about my age but they had fishing nets, and jamjars with handles made of string to carry them. The jamjars were full of pinkeens swimming around, and the nets were made of the tops of nylons, with a wire going around inside and stuck into a handle made of bamboo that was like the canes the teachers used at school. They tied a knot in the stocking and cut the rest off. After I saw them the first few times I asked my mother if I could have one of her old nylons to make a net, but she said no. We had real fishing nets my father got us in Hector Grey's, that we used when we went out in the car on picnics. We used to catch pinkeens in a river up the mountains, but we always had to throw them back before we came home.

For a long time I didn't know where the boys with the jamjars and the fishing nets were coming from. Once I nearly asked them, but one of them said "Are you looking, young one?" and I had to run away. But that was when I was small. I thought they must have walked all the way down from the mountains.

By the time I was bigger I knew where they came from. There was a park with a river, called the Woods, because there were trees all along by the banks. We used to go there sometimes, with my mother pushing the twins in the pram and me and Eugene walking along beside, but we didn't go near the water. It was muddy down there and the pram would get stuck. Anyway I think there were sometimes boys swimming with only their underpants.

There was only one place I was allowed to go near the river, a place with no trees so my mother could see me from where she was sitting on the grass. You had to swing on a big gate across a sort of swamp to get there, and on the other side there were only children. People always had their shoes and socks off down there. You could see pinkeens swimming around between the stones, but Eugene was too small to go across on the gate, so I was always on my own. I used to feel stupid with nobody to play with and not even a jamjar, so the next day I usually stayed in the back lane.

The worst thing about the back lane was when the Walshes went on their holidays. They were the people I usually played with, so when there were only the little ones it was useless. I used to have all my library books read and my mother would keep telling me to go out in the fresh air but I didn't want to because any game I tried to play, the little ones would just mess it up. So I used to hang around the house all day and give out about everything. My mother would get annoyed and then when my father came home he'd give out to me and tell me I didn't know how lucky I was. When my mother was my age she had to milk cows but she didn't sit around moping in the house when the sun was shining and I was to go out. But where was I supposed to go? There was only the back lane and up to the shops.

One day they said if I didn't have manners and be cheerful they'd write to my Auntie Tess and tell her not to send Teresa. I didn't know what they were talking about.

I knew who Auntie Tess was of course. Uncle Bob was my mother's brother and she was married to him. They lived in Templegarve with Granda and my cousins, and Auntie Tess came to our house the time Granny was in hospital. Teresa was my cousin but I hadn't ever seen her. They called her the baby, even though she was a year older than me. She had three big brothers and no sisters and now she was coming to stay in our house for a week. My mother showed me the letter from Auntie Tess that said Bob has to go up to Dublin on Thursday and he will drop her off then, D.V.

Eugene had to move into the little bed in the twins' room so Teresa could have his bed. I was really excited. We could have midnight feasts and pillow fights like in books, but mostly I thought we'd be allowed out on our own, because Teresa was nearly eleven. Lots of children younger than me used to go to the park on their own, but I wasn't allowed until I was ten, and I had someone sensible to go with. Teresa would be somebody sensible. They knew her mother and father and we even had the same Granda. She was from the country, and at school they always said country people were much wiser than us. They knew all about making hay and the work of the blacksmith. I thought probably Teresa would have a pet lamb at home that she fed with a baby's bottle, or some other animal that she'd rescued.

The first day she arrived she hardly said anything. She had on a blue dress with white ankle socks and black patent shoes, and blue ribbons on her plaits that exactly matched her dress. I couldn't imagine her on a farm. Uncle Bob only stayed for a cup of tea, then he gave her a pound and told her to be a good girl. He gave me half a crown to share with Eugene.

When my Dad came home we had our real tea and then we all went down town in the car because Teresa had never been in Dublin before. I couldn't believe it. The next day it turned out she had only been on a bus twice in her life and never on a double-decker. She came out and looked at the back lane. I showed her the hopscotch I'd made before the Walshes went on their holidays, but she didn't want to play.

She wanted to go up to the shops all the time and buy ice-pops, and cross at the traffic lights and look at the televisions in McCann's window. She didn't know anything about the work of the blacksmith, and she said she hated farming. She said you'd want to be a real eejit to marry a farmer. She was going to do a commercial course. She wouldn't marry anyone who couldn't afford to bring her to the pictures at least once a week. She had her good blue dress and another dress with stripes, and she wore one of them every day going to Mass. She never went to Mass on weekdays at home. The church was four miles away and there were only two Masses on Sunday. She didn't have any nuns in her school either, only a lady teacher and a man teacher. There were only two classrooms in the whole school and boys and girls in the same class. The teacher never said anything to them about guardian angels or occasion of sin, and they were allowed to wear anything they liked.

Teresa changed into her shorts every day when we came home from Mass. I was worried about it at the beginning, but we went up to the shops every day and nobody said anything to her. The weather was getting warm so I put on my shorts too.

I was right about one thing: we were allowed to go to the park by ourselves as long as we were home by five o'clock and we didn't go into the Woods. We had to stay near the swings and not speak to strangers except when we thought it was nearly time to go home, and then we had to say "Excuse me, have you got the right time, please?"

The swings were great. I was getting good at swinging really high, but I showed Teresa where the gate was for going across to the river and then she wanted to go.

I said, "But we're not allowed."

"Don't be such a stupid eejit," she said, so we went.

We took off our sandals, and paddled. It wasn't like in the sea: there was mud on the bottom that came up in little clouds between your toes. We just dried our feet on the grass and put on our sandals again. They felt lovely and cool. Two boys came past us with fishing nets and jamjars full of pinkeens, and one of them said "Are you looking?" but Teresa just laughed. I started to laugh as well and they walked on.

At home eating our tea Teresa asked my mother if we could go fishing. She said, "Auntie Molly, there's two fishing nets in the shed and there's a place in the Woods you can catch pinkeens."

My mother looked at me. I knew I was going red. I said, "We only went to the place beside the gate," but she didn't give out. She put more cocktail sausages on the table. "If you take the fishing nets, you'll have to promise not to go anywhere except near the gate, and only go up to your knees in the water."

I couldn't believe we were really allowed to go. After tea I went rooting for string and I put handles on two big jamjars. I got my Dad to help me with the knots so they would be good and strong.


The next day was really hot. After dinner we got our jamjars and my mother gave Eugene something to do so he wouldn't see us taking the fishing nets. I was a bit ashamed that we didn't have the proper kind made out of nylons, but Teresa said ours were better. The fish wouldn't be able to see them.

Every other day going to the park, Teresa bought an ice-pop with her money, but this day we just walked right past Mooney's and I was glad. She always gave me a bite, but when she was finished she always held onto her stick till we came to the post-box on the corner near the park, then she posted it in. They had different post-boxes down the country, she told me, stuck into the wall, not roundy ones like ours. I was afraid the postman would come to empty it when we were passing, and find all the ice-pop sticks.

We didn't even stop at the swings. We just went straight down to the river. It was awkward swinging across on the gate with the nets and the jamjars, but we managed all right, and anyway the ground underneath was nearly dry because the weather was so warm. There were people already fishing at our place but Teresa just went straight along to a big flat rock that was nearly in the woods but not really. She took off her sandals and went right in.

Our nets were really good for catching pinkeens because the handles were so long. We threw back all the tiny ones and kept the big ones in the jars. Even the boys that said "Are you looking?" the other day came to look at them. Other people said hello, or some of them just smiled. Peter Mooney from Mooney's shop passed by a few times and I said hello to him. I don't think he knew me because he didn't say anything the first time. I only knew him because his father and mother had the shop and I was supposed to say hello to the neighbours, but he didn't really live there. He only came on visits, but I knew him because he looked like Frank, and Frank worked in the shop.

We stayed fishing in the same place for ages. We kept catching pinkeens but they weren't as big as the ones we had in the jars, so we kept throwing them back. Teresa wanted to go further down the river but I said we weren't allowed and she told me I was an eejit. We were just nearly having a fight when Peter Mooney came past again and asked us if he could look at our fish. He said they were very good but he knew a place where there were bigger ones. He said they didn't like the sunlight so you had to go to a shady place. He'd show us if we liked.

Teresa said "All right." She wanted to go into the woods but we weren't allowed unless we had an adult with us. If

Peter Mooney wasn't there she probably would have made me go anyway. He walked down the path and we walked behind him. Then he said "This is the place," and Teresa said really loud "Where are they?"

"Ssh!" he said. "You have to be very quiet and not move." He was whispering.

He told us to stand in the water. He stood behind us, but he didn't take off his shoes and socks. He put his hand on my shoulder and made me lean against him. He was pointing at the water but I couldn't see anything. He kept saying "Ssh!" and then he said "There they are!" but he was rubbing my leg with his thumb. It rubbed softly at first, but then really hard, right up inside my shorts.

I didn't want to say anything in case I'd disturb the fish, but I was glad when he took his thumb away. I thought maybe he was so interested in the pinkeens he forgot it was there, but I was afraid to move and it was beginning to hurt me. I still couldn't see any fish and my feet were very cold in the water. Peter Mooney wasn't saying anything so in the end I said, "We have to go home now."

I thought it must be late because it was so dark under the trees and the water was so cold, but when we came back to the place near the gate the sun was still shining and there were people still fishing. Some of them were throwing stones in the water, making big bright splashes. Teresa said "Do you want to fish some more?" but I said no.

Our jamjars were full of fish and we didn't want to spill the water, so we couldn't go across on the gate. I climbed down into the swampy place and Teresa handed me the jars. Then she climbed down and we walked across sort of stepping-stones in the mud. We stopped at the swings for a little while, but then it was time to go home. We had to walk very slowly so the water wouldn't all splash out, and I started to get really annoyed. It was the second time I couldn't move because of the stupid pinkeens.

When we got as far as the post-box on the corner I told Teresa to wait for me.

"What are you doing?" she asked me.

"Nothing," I said. I sat down on the kerb, then I got my net and I poured the whole jar of pinkeens into it. They were all jumping and twitching on top of one another. I got up and posted them into the letter-box. Some of them fell on the ground but I picked them up and posted them in too, covered in dust. Teresa said, "You'll be killed," but I said, "I don't care."

I was able to run nearly all the way home. Teresa had to walk slowly because of her fish, but I waited for her at the bottom of the road. My father asked me at teatime "What about you, Una? Did you not catch any pinkeens?"

"I did," I said, "I got a whole lot, but I didn't want to carry them."

# LEMON GRASS

James and Lydia give a dinner party every week. They spend all day Saturday preparing it, and all Saturday evening serving it and eating. They never get fat. They're savouring this meal, tearing off pieces of bread, greedily mopping up the last delicious dollops of sauce, talking animatedly to Ronnie and Annette and James' mother, Maura.

They usually have six people, but tonight some man from Lydia's London office couldn't make it. Lydia apologised to Maura when she arrived, as though the nameless colleague had been a treat in store for her, but Maura simply smiled. She knows by now that's all Lydia expects of her.

James and Lydia each wriggle with pleasure as the other appears from the kitchen with more food. With their blond hair and lightly freckled skin they look more like brother and sister than husband and wife, but James has blue eyes, and Lydia's are green.

The soup is intriguing, creamy but tangy, and there are prawns in it. Apprehensive, Annette watches Ronnie tasting it. He looks around beatifically after the first spoonful, his glasses all foggy from the steam. Peanuts, she thinks, and lemon.

"It's a peanut soup," James says, "with prawns. And there's lemon and garlic and scallions and stuff as well."

The vegetables for their main course are lightly steamed and tossed with sesame oil. The meat is delicate and pale. "Veal," guesses Ronnie, joining in the game, but "No," James and Lydia grin, delighted with their innocent deception, "it's turkey!"

"Cilantro," says Lydia—that's what the flavour is— "Quinnsworth have it in Merrion. It's wonderful, isn't it?"

"Marvellous," says Annette, "Cilantro, did you say? What does it look like?"

James has disappeared. He comes back smiling from the kitchen, and lays in front of Annette something that looks like dusty wilted parsley. "It's the leaves of the coriander plant," he says. "Some recipes say use parsley if you can't get cilantro, but really there's no comparison."

"I thought it looked a bit like parsley myself," Maura says. The others turn kindly and look at her. She certainly is wonderful. So independent! She doesn't bat an eyelid. Even learned to drive at sixty, after her husband died. Not many people's mothers would come along like this and eat whatever was served up to them, spicy food and foreign flavours, and not a potato in sight.

"What I would really like to get hold of," Lydia is telling Annette, "is lemon grass."

James serves coffee in front of the fire, in tiny exquisite cups from a shop in Francis Street. He and Lydia smile at compliments on their wonderful food and their beautiful house, and Annette smiles too, watching them. She didn't expect to like them, after hearing so much from Ronnie. Of course their house is lovely. Of course they do things properly. They have two jobs, and no kids. What is there to stop them? But now she finds she does like them. She feels pampered and appreciated, and James, standing in front of his mother with cream and brown sugar, is sweetly boyish without his suit and tie. Lydia, she thinks, is probably shy in spite of being so poised.

On Sunday morning Lydia, clear-headed, gets up first and makes coffee. She goes out for the papers while James starts the washing-up. He admires the way she moves aloofly through the chaos of congealing sauces and crumpled napkins as though none of it has anything to do with her. Plunging his bare arms among the floating fragments in the sink makes him feel like a troubadour. She is his lady and he is her swain. She'd laugh if she knew what he was thinking.

When the house is clean again they sit in their soft armchairs, reading book reviews and business news.

"A walk?" James asks after lunch. He throws the car keys to Lydia and they head for the Pine Forest.

They do have a nice life, and striding past families with wailing children makes James appreciate it even more. They congratulate each other from time to time on the harmony they've created, but mostly they walk in silence. The grass at the edges of the forest path is fine and shiny, casting wispy shadows in the spring sun. "Lemon grass," James thinks, "what on earth is lemon grass?"

On Sundays they both wear jeans and running shoes, and Lydia leaves her hair loose. Now as they walk, the sun comes slanting between trees and shines right through it. It looks like sunbeams, or magic silk, but James doesn't tell her. She doesn't like silly love-talk, except when it's her idea. Sometimes she comes wrapped in her soft blue dressing gown after a bath and snuggles on a cushion at his feet, but he knows if he tried being playful now she'd frown—or give that little laugh of hers. It's important to Lydia that they're grown up, so James thinks about the children they'll have some day and stores up his magic princess thoughts for them instead.

"Maybe when you're in London you can pick up some of that lemon grass," he says, back in the car. Lydia seems more preoccupied than usual. He's trying to jolly her along, but subtly.

"Hm?"

"In London. This week. I thought you could get some of that lemon grass stuff you were talking about."

"Lemon grass? What? Oh, yes, maybe."

I'll miss you, he wants to say. Are you looking forward to going? I hope you'll enjoy it. It won't be all work. Four days. I'll miss you. But Lydia's looking straight ahead as she drives, deep in her own thoughts.

Maura clears up her lunch dishes and decides to go to Dún Laoghaire.

At the end of the east pier she stops just long enough to look out to sea, then turns back. This is the best part of the walk. The wind's behind her and she likes this view of the land, with the Victorian terraces spread out so proudly across the seafront. It reminds her of coming home on the boat from

Wales with Jim. She imagines she's re-entering her life, coming back from somewhere else.

A family is walking towards her. A red-haired man with glasses and a small dark woman, both with their hands in their pockets, a big dog on a lead, and two little girls with red, wind-blown faces and their mother's dark curls, running in circles around their parents.

She smiles at them, but the young woman speaks, "Maura?" she says.

"Oh, hello. It's Annette, isn't it? And Ronnie. How are you?" She takes off her mitten to shake hands. Ronnie smiles at her, "And these are our two rascals."

"Orla," he calls, "Clare. Come on, we're going back. Say hello to Mrs Halpin."

Orla, the smaller girl, grins at her, "Our dog is called Séamus," she says. "He's a golden retriever."

"Do you live in Dún Laoghaire?" Ronnie asks.

"No, I'm in Rathfarnham," Maura smiles at the child, strokes the dog's silky head, "but I love the sea."

"We're just up the road," Annette says. "At least, not too far. We usually walk down the west pier, but the kids like this one better."

"I try to get out for a walk every Sunday," Maura tells them. She laughs, "I'm lucky to have the car. Anything is better than sitting looking out at the bricks."

Annette walks beside her, suddenly struck by a vision of sitting all day in a silent house.

"Would you like to come up with us for a cup of tea?" she asks hesitantly when they get back to the bandstand.

"I'd love to," Maura says, "as long as you don't go to any trouble."

"No trouble at all," Ronnie says, "Orla, hold Mrs Halpin's hand crossing the road."

"If you like," says Annette, when Maura has admired the shambling comfort of their big untidy house, "we could feed the kids and get them off to bed, and then the three of us could sit down in peace. You could light us a fire in the sitting room, couldn't you, Love?"

Maura helps the children off with their coats and fills Séamus's bowl with water. Ronnie bustles in and out with briquettes and firelighters and Annette grills fish fingers for the children's tea.

"That was a wonderful meal last night, wasn't it? I think Lydia's amazing."

"Yes," Maura says, "Lydia is amazing," and something in her voice makes Annette turn to look at her.

"Did she grow up in Ireland?" she asks. A leading question, but she's curious, and Maura looks happier here in her kitchen than she did in her own son's dining-room last night.

"Oh yes," Maura laughs. "She grew up in County Clare."

Annette feels herself blush. "I just thought, the way she speaks. And with a name like Lydia."

"Her mother got it out of a book. She's a great reader."

"I never met her properly before last night—so I never heard anything about her parents. I knew James of course, through Ronnie."

"They're very nice people, Lydia's parents," Maura says, and carries the tray of cups and saucers into the sitting room.

She comes back smiling, "You know, they have a huge family down there—nine of them—Lydia's the youngest, and they're all completely down-to-earth. You'd be surprised. When Lydia and James got married I remember they had a champagne toast for the bride and groom—but Lydia's brothers all had bottles of stout instead." Both the women laugh. Ronnie comes into the kitchen and they busy themselves seriously. When the phone rings and he leaves to answer it, they smile at each other, admitting complicity.

"To tell you the truth," Maura says, "I don't feel I know her very well myself—but then I'm the mother-in-law. I'm probably the worst kind too." She laughs, "I'd love to have grandchildren. I don't say a word of course, but I'm afraid she senses it and she doesn't like it. James was my only one. He's very happy though, and that's the main thing."

"It is," says Annette, "it certainly is."


After speaking to Ronnie on the upstairs phone, Lydia comes down and walks out to the garden. James is peering at his herb-bed in the dusk, waiting for the seedlings to appear. Lydia saw him from the window before she made the call.

"I have to go in to the office for a while," she says. "Sort out a few things before I go to London."


Maura's still in the kitchen with Annette when the doorbell rings. Ronnie has been putting the girls to bed and they hear him come downstairs, but instead of going to answer it he turns in the hall and comes down the three more steps. Apologetically, he looks around the door: "Maura, I'm afraid that's Lydia at the door and I think she's upset, so if you don't mind I won't let on you're here."

Maura looks at Annette, but she's equally puzzled and mimes an elaborate shrug as they hunch silently over the table, ears pricked to hear Lydia's voice at the hall door.

Ronnie follows Lydia into the empty sitting room, cosy with firelight. He hears the echo of his own voice saying "I think she's upset," and wonders why he said it. Her blonde hair is combed smooth and pulled back into a flat clip, and her shoulders are straight. Ronnie has never seen her upset—beside her, James the sunny optimist looks like a dithering neurotic—but he's never seen her alone either. He can't imagine why suddenly she needs to talk to him.

"Sit down," he says, aware of the tray of cups and saucers on the low table. He moves them over by the window. Lydia still hasn't said anything. When he sits down opposite her in the other big armchair she takes a deep breath.

"I want you to do me a favour."

"Of course."

"It's because you're James' friend. The favour is for him."

Ronnie sits in silence, puzzled.

"I'm going to leave him, but I'm afraid it'll be a shock to him."

It's a shock to Ronnie, and he looks at her calm, aristocratic face for a clue. "But, do you mean he won't accept it? He hasn't said anything to me about it. I'd no idea you two were having problems. I'm really sorry to hear it." He's babbling now. Shut up, Ronnie.

"I haven't told him yet," Lydia says.

"You what?" Ronnie is aghast, then relieved. "Oh, I thought by the way you said it you'd really made up your mind."

"I have," says Lydia, and Ronnie stares at her. He can see now that her composure is a kind of frantic armour.

"When?" he asks gently, the way he might approach a frightened, dangerous animal.

"Tomorrow morning," she answers, and he feels his mouth go dry. His head begins to float.

"You're going to tell him tomorrow morning or you're leaving tomorrow morning?"

"Leaving," she says, faltering for the first time.

"You're leaving James tomorrow morning and you haven't told him yet?" Ronnie is both angry and very scared.

"I'll ring him from London," she says.

"Look," says Ronnie, "maybe I'm being very stupid, but I think you'd better explain all that to me again."

"I've got a new job," Lydia says, "in the London office, and I'm going tomorrow. I've got a flat fixed up there as well, and I'll have enough clothes with me so I won't need to come back here till James has time to get used to the idea. I've made all the arrangements, so there won't have to be any scenes."

"But what about James?"

"He thinks I'm just going for a few days. I'll ring him tomorrow night."

"I mean, why didn't you talk to him? I'm sure if he knew you had your heart set on London he'd go too. He's crazy about you, you know."

"Yes," says Lydia, "I know. That's why I don't want any discussion. It'll be much better if I just go." She tosses her head proudly and Ronnie thinks he sees the tiniest glint of tears in her eyes, "I know I'm the one in the wrong, so he can just have all the furniture and everything. My clothes are all clean and they're all together in the wardrobe. I've left everything tidy."

"What was that stuff you said you wanted?" Ronnie asks, hypnotised by her icy tale, like a chicken with its beak on a white line.

"What stuff?"

"Some stuff last night, for cooking. Some kind of grass."

"Oh, lemon grass. They use it in Thai cooking. It was just something to say." She's looking at him hard, even impatiently.

"So anyway, I was hoping you might keep an eye on James for a few days. Give him a ring or something?" She stands up, waiting for him to stand too.

Ronnie opens the door of the sitting room, and she walks past him into the hall. What would he do, he asks himself, if this was a story? Whack the back of her neck with one swift sideways blow, or invite her to stay for tea? Phone James? Delay her here and do something to her car? He knows he won't do anything. People don't. Afterwards, when it's all over, he'll probably talk about it. When it turns into a story he might make some sense of it. He watches Lydia walk the few yards to the gate, then closes the front door and walks heavily down the three steps to where Annette and Maura are waiting behind the closed kitchen door.

# SECRET PASSAGES

I suppose the knobs on the banister were to stop you sliding down. A whole lot of little wooden knobs sticking up out of it all the way down. I used to try to count them but I always got a different answer. Sometimes our line was stopped on the stairs waiting for another class to come back from the toilets and I could get up to about thirty-nine, but then we had to start moving again. I always lost count where the stairs curved round at the bottom.

All the things in books, like sliding down the banisters and discovering secret passages, we couldn't do them. Robbing orchards was the same: boys used to talk about robbing orchards, but there was always glass on top of the walls. Broken glass stuck into concrete. I didn't see how they could.

If our school was in a book you'd twist one of the knobs on the banister, then a panel would open and you'd find a secret passage or a priest's hole.

There were panels on the walls in a lot of places, in our last year's classroom and the cookery room and part of the corridor and the old stairs. But there only looked like enough space for the wall between two classrooms, and if you looked up from outside there was always the right number of windows. I used to twist the knobs anyway, going down the stairs. Not that I really expected to find a priest's hole in a convent, but it was worth trying.

We had a cross teacher. She always brought her cane with her when we went out in our line and you could get slapped for fidgeting. We were supposed to walk along in single file with our hands down by our sides and not talk. You could say aspirations under your breath—there were notices on the stairs that said *November Pray for the Holy Souls*—but you couldn't talk to anyone. If you said enough aspirations you could get a soul out of Purgatory.

I would say I was one of the medium bold girls. Not one of the really bold ones. They always got everything wrong and they were always late. They had a real Dublin accent and they sometimes came to school without their books or they had no pencil. But I wasn't one of the goody-goodies either, with their finger on their lips and their other finger wagging at you or saying "Ohee ohee ohee. I'm telling the nun," or "Ohee ohee ohee, I'm telling on you," if it was a lady teacher instead of a nun. Anyway that's why I was so surprised when a girl came in on a message and told Miss Keegan I was wanted in the office. I wasn't in trouble with Miss Keegan so I didn't see how I could be in trouble with the head nun.

Outside the door of our classroom I pulled my socks up, then I walked down to the end of the corridor and around the corner. The door of the office was open and the head nun told me to come in. She smiled at me. I thought some other teacher must be there, or someone's mother, but there was nobody.

All the big black roll books from all the classes were on her desk and one of them was open. I could see my name upside down. Una Fitzsimons. There was a whole row of red ticks beside it and no duck eggs like some people had. I was never sick except one time in High Babies when I had the measles.

Two girls in my class were delicate. They never came to school if it was raining and they only had to put up their hand to go out to the toilet anytime on their own. The rest of us had to wait and go out in the line. If anyone who wasn't delicate stayed home from school on a wet day the teacher said they were a sugar baby. Some other people used to mitch, but our house was near the school, so I always ended up going. I liked school anyway, especially when we had Sister Flavian, before we got Miss Keegan. She was lovely and young. You could really imagine her with hair, and proper lady's clothes.

When I was small and someone told me nuns were women, I didn't believe them. I thought they were men because they didn't have hair or lipstick or nylons or high heels. But you'd know Sister Flavian was a woman. Her veil was different from the other nuns' and her frock didn't go all the way down to the ground. You could see part of her legs and shoes and stockings, and at the sides of her head you could see black curly hair and part of her ears. She was a lovely singer as well. She hardly ever slapped anyone, and once a girl in my class whose mother was dead wrote me a note that said: "Sister Flavian is my real mother."

It was hard to imagine the head nun was a woman, even though I knew she must be. But she didn't look like a man either. She wasn't a bit like Sister Flavian anyway. I watched her looking back through the pages of the roll, saying something to herself. I was pretty sure I wasn't going to get slapped, but I still didn't know what she wanted me for. My socks were slipping down, but I didn't dare pull them up. I was just hoping she wasn't going to tell me I had a vocation. We had an old nun for sewing—she had crooked fingers and a big hard nail on her thumb. She was always telling us God might be calling us, but I didn't want to be a nun.

The head nun didn't say anything about a vocation. She closed the roll and looked at me.

"Well Una," she said, "have you been a good girl?"

I didn't know if she meant me to say yes, or if that would be giving cheek, but I thought I'd better not say no. I said "I don't know."

"You haven't missed any day this year, have you?"

"No, Sister."

"You haven't got television at home, have you?"

"No, Sister."

"No," she said, "good."

Every time someone was sent to the office for not having their home exercise done, the nun asked them if they had television.

The next thing, she took a huge big key out of the drawer in her desk and said to me, "I want you to be in charge of this key."

It was like Thou art Peter and upon this rock I will build my church and I will give to thee the keys of the Kingdom of Heaven. I didn't know what the key was for. I was afraid it was maybe a vocation after all.

My socks were all the way down to my ankles. "Yes, Sister," I said. I was getting used to the office: I could read the lists stuck to the wall, with the teachers' names and what classrooms they were in, and I could see out the window onto the white flowers of a cherry tree in a garden next door to the school.

"I want you to lock the gate every morning and bring the key up here to me in the office. Will you do that?"

"Yes, Sister." I didn't know if she meant the big black gate at the front of the school, but I couldn't think of any other gate. I never even knew it was locked when we were in school, but I suppose if it wasn't, people could get out.

"You'll go upstairs with your line as usual so Miss Keegan can mark you present, but then you'll come straight here to the office for the key. Is that clear?"

"Yes, Sister."

"Have you got a watch?"

"No, Sister."

"No, well. You'll hear the bell on the chapel ringing at a quarter-to-ten. When you hear that bell you're to lock the gate and bring the key up here to me. Can you be trusted to do that?"

"Yes, Sister."

"Good child. Now go back to your class and come here to me first thing tomorrow morning."

"Yes, Sister."

I came out of the office and walked a bit slowly so I could think about the key and the gate and the office. I stopped a few times to pull up my socks. I was hardly ever out in the corridor by myself. We were always in our line for going to the toilets and going home, and every morning and every day after lunch we had to stay in the playground till the head nun came out and rang a bell. Then everyone had to get into their own line and go upstairs with their teacher.

When I got back to the class the girl beside me asked what I was wanted in the office for, but Miss Keegan told her to stop talking and I was just as glad. I didn't know what people would say if they knew I had the job of locking us all in.

I didn't tell my mother about it when I went home either, but I went to the drawer and got out some elastic and a needle and thread. I made myself a new pair of garters, with stitches, not knots, so my socks would stay up.

The first time I had to lock the gate I was really nervous. I'd hardly ever used any kind of key before and I wasn't even sure it was the right gate, but I heard the bell on the chapel and there wasn't anybody coming in late. I just pushed the two sides of the big black gate until they closed, then I turned the key in the lock and it worked.

Coming back up the driveway was like having no clothes on—I didn't want anyone to see me but my skin felt different. I wanted to twirl around and let the wind blow under my arms. I walked in near the wall so no one would see me out the windows and I did twirl around a little bit.

That was the part I liked best every day after that—coming up the driveway after I'd locked the gate—especially past where there was sort of a field and you could see the nuns' garden on the other side.

The garden was lovely but we only saw it when the May procession was on, except sometimes if our line was stopped near a window upstairs. You could see nuns' giant underwear on clotheslines from there, but it was too far to see flowers.

For the May procession we all got out of our classes. We had to wear white dresses and veils, and go through a special door near where *November Pray for the Holy Souls* was, down a long dark passage and through a shed. Then we came out in the sunshine. We walked slowly two by two around all the paths between the vegetables, singing hymns and saying decades of the Rosary, around the flowerbeds and under the trees.

We sang "I'll sing a hymn to Mary, the mother of my God, the virgin of all virgins of David's royal blood," and "O Mary, we crown thee with blossoms today, queen of the angels and queen of the May."

The best thing was we really did crown her. There was a statue of Our Lady in the garden and the end of the procession was always somebody climbing up and putting a crown of flowers on her head. It used to make me think it might be nice to have a vocation and be a nun after all.

I spent so much time dawdling up the driveway in the mornings after I locked the gate that I always had to hurry on the stairs and in the corridor. I was afraid if I was late the nun would take the job away from me, so I never managed to count the knobs on the banister or twist them or tap all the places on the panelling like I thought I would.

People got to know me locking the gate. The warden used to be just going home, coming out the side door after leaving in his sign and his white coat and cap, and every time he saw me coming with the key he'd say, "Here comes St Peter!"

There was a woman as well, rushing up with her little girl nearly every day just before I locked the gate. I knew her name was Mrs Brown, but I didn't let on I knew. Her little girl was in High Babies and she must have got into trouble every day for being late, but her mother was always really cheerful. She nearly always said something to me.

Some days I used to pretend things, like holding onto the bars of the gate and pretending I was a gorilla in the zoo or a condemned prisoner. Once after I locked the gate, I opened it again with the key just to see what it would be like. I imagined just walking out and going somewhere, but I didn't.

One morning I was turning the key in the lock and Noreen Brown was running up the driveway behind me. Her mother was outside, looking in through the bars and waving. Suddenly she said to me "Is that Sister Flavian? Hasn't she got very thin?" I looked around and it was Sister Flavian, coming along the path from the convent part. I hadn't seen her for a long time, but I never knew if people had got thin or fat.

When I finished locking the gate she was standing there, waiting for me to walk up the driveway.

"How are you, Una?" she said, and "Isn't it a lovely day?" and a few things like that. I was trying not to walk too fast. Then Sister Flavian said "You're a great reader, aren't you?"

I wondered how she knew that. I was always being given out to at home for having my nose stuck in a book, but she didn't sound as if she was giving out. Then she asked me "What books do you like best?"

I looked up and she was smiling. I thought I might as well tell the truth. "Enid Blyton," I said.

"Oh," she said, then something I didn't hear properly, then, "Did you ever read a book called *The Lion, the Witch and the Wardrobe*?" I think that was the name she said.

I said no.

"You should look for it," she said, "it's very good."

It sounded really babyish, but I didn't want to hurt her feelings. I said I'd see if it was in the library. I was a bit disappointed. I thought maybe she was going to tell me something good I could read. All the books at home were things like *David Copperfield* and *Kidnapped*, that I'd read ages ago, or else ones I wasn't allowed to read. At school they were always giving out about comics, but the only other thing you ever heard about was the *Imeldist*. I was beginning to get a bit tired of Enid Blyton, so it would have been nice to know something else that was good besides Nancy Drew and the Bobbsey twins.

Still, I was glad to see Sister Flavian again. She must have been away studying or praying. My mother said the different veil and the short skirt meant she was still a novice. They had to spend a long time studying and praying before they were sure they really had a vocation, then they took their final vows and got proper nun's clothes. Now she was back there was maybe a chance we'd have her again next year. It wouldn't be so bad to still be in National School. She always used to say she liked our class.

I was feeling cheerful when I went back to Miss Keegan's class. I sent a note to my friend Marian that I'd seen Sister Flavian.

But that time I met her on the driveway was only a few days before I saw the green car. I was coming into school one morning and a man in a green car was asking the warden for directions. Then the car turned in the gate of the convent. Usually only priests' cars went in that gate in the morning, and they were always black.

The real reason I remember it, though, is that I saw it again that same day at a quarter to ten when I was locking the gate. Sister Flavian was in it, only she wasn't Sister Flavian any more. She was wearing a red coat and no veil.

I didn't believe it could be her even though I saw her face and the black curly hair, but then she waved to me as the car passed by so I knew it must be. I waved back through the bars.

Walking up the driveway with the key after the green car disappeared, I felt really annoyed. I knew we definitely wouldn't have Sister Flavian next year and I wished I could just leave and go to secondary at the end of this year. I was fed up going everywhere in a stupid line and being locked in. I knew I'd never find any secret passages in that school. I knew I definitely didn't want to be a nun and I wasn't even looking forward to the May procession. My Communion dress was going to be too small anyway. I thought I might look for the book about the lion and the witch and the wardrobe after all, but I didn't know who'd written it and I wasn't sure that was even its name, and the worst thing was I couldn't think of anyone I could ask.

# BLUE MURDER

Going home on the bike in the smoggy dark, I watch out for potholes, and car doors flying open. People get killed all the time. Once on my way over to Paul's last summer, when I hadn't known him all that long, I realised I wasn't carrying anything that could identify me. All I had in my front basket were two cream buns that I'd baked, and a hacksaw he'd lent me. I remember us lying in bed that day with the sun on our skin, making jokes about that, but it was one of the reasons I gave him keys to my place. Living alone can scare you. There were other reasons too, of course, to do with lying in bed, and laughing, but as the days have got shorter and colder and darker, they seem to have gone further and further away.

His bike isn't there when I lock mine to the railings, and the front window is dark. Before I knew Paul, I used to hate coming home to the empty flat, but now when I open the big hall door I suddenly have this great flooding feeling of peace and possibility. There's a light under Alice and Joanie's door, but no sound, and I know Alice is probably in there by herself, correcting copybooks. My own room even looks nice when I light the small lamp instead of the one overhead, and I potter around, tidying up. I put on a tape of Emmylou Harris, and waltz in and out from the kitchen to the table, singing to the toast about only going over Jordan, singing to my scrambled eggs that I'm only going over home.

Later I'm sitting reading by the gas fire, in a little warm pool of light from the lamp over the bed, when the phone rings in the hall and Alice knocks on my door. I talk to Paul: he's having a drink in town, but he'll be out later. He's phoning from a pub and it's noisy, so we don't have any conversation, but I go back to sit by the fire and all I can think of, looking at it, is that that would be a good way for Paul to do me in. He could sneak out of bed some night and turn it on without lighting it. I'm such a heavy sleeper I wouldn't notice a thing. He could just pull the door after him and go.

I never used to think about anyone killing me, only about accidents. It worries me, how much I think about it. Ever since Halloween. Paul went home to his family, and I know something happened, but he won't tell me what. He says it's not my problem and I wouldn't understand, but he hardly ever goes back to his own place now. He stays at the flat nearly every night, and yet whole evenings go by when he hardly speaks to me. I know it's not good, but if I even think about saying anything to him, my mind shies away like a horse refusing a jump, all huge and heaving, and my stomach goes to pieces. The glass panel beside the cooker is still broken from the time he punched his fist into it, and I keep seeing that thin transparent orangey film of blood.

I can't concentrate on my book after he rings. I've been so jittery lately. If I stay up, he'll probably say I was lying in wait for him. I could take a bath and go to bed though, and I'd be relaxed when he comes in. Usually I take showers at the gym because of that bathroom. It's just a box tacked onto the outside of the house, so it's always freezing, and the only water heater is an ancient gas geyser. But a bath does seem like a good idea. I give the water plenty of time to run, and I leave the door open to let the place warm up. I cut an old empty Badedas bottle open with scissors and it makes more bubbles than I expected.

I'm reading in bed, wearing my big warm nightdress, when Paul comes in. He's a bit drunk, I can see; cheerful enough, but even so he stands as if he's wearing something heavy.

I'm all rosy and glowing though; I grin at him.

"What are you so happy about?"

"Nothing, I just had a nice hot bath."

"A bath, eh?" He walks into the bathroom, then out and over to the bookcase. He takes out a couple of books; puts them back. "It's still warm in there. Maybe I should have a bath myself."

"Go ahead if you want to," I say. My voice tastes sour in my mouth. I turn out the lamp and pull the blankets over my shoulders. I watch him in the light from the bathroom, coming in and out, dropping his shoes and his clothes at the bottom of the bed. He's so thin. He closes the door and I hear him sloshing around in there. I hunch down in the dark, wondering what's going to happen; whether he'll expect to find me asleep or awake when he comes out. The rosy glow of my bath is wearing away and the sick coldness is starting in my stomach again.

There's a sound from the bathroom—one long sliding splash. I listen hard, sitting up. A sort of gurgle, then nothing.

"Paul!" I call. Then with that awful, weightless, breathless feeling, I get to the door and bang on it. He's locked it, but it's only a small stupid bolt and it breaks. The smell of gas is suffocating. Paul's face is half in the water and his eyes are closed. I start screaming for Alice or Joanie, and I manage to hold his face above the water while I turn off the gas. As I crouch there, holding his wet and heavy head, and Alice comes blundering into the room outside, I feel myself turning into feathers and lead. Half of my brain is somewhere on the ceiling, looking down admiringly at my devotion. The other half is sick and racing like a rat inside my head, but inside my stomach, down near the floor, there's a dark, heavy lump of anger. This is it, Paul, something is saying, behind my clenched teeth. You've gone too far this time, it says. And I am finished.

Alice helps me to drag him out, and we lay him on the floor. I'm not gibbering or crying, but I still can't get my breath properly. I know we should call an ambulance, but I can't leave Paul. His breathing is really strange and I'm afraid he'll die if I turn my back. Alice is doing the real work. We hear the hall door and she yells to whoever it is, "Get an ambulance." Joanie puts her head in, and when I hear her on the phone I start to breathe. Alice has Paul on his side, with blankets over him. He groans a little, but his eyes are still closed.

Joanie comes in and puts her arm around me. She doesn't ask what happened. "The ambulance is coming," she says, "You'll be okay. Are those your jeans? Put them on. Have you got a warm sweater? Do you need a loan of some money? Where are your keys?"

I move slowly. I do everything she tells me.

"Do you want us to come with you?" Alice asks.

"No," I shake my head. "Thanks." I try to look at both of them. A blue light flashes outside the window and Joanie goes to open the hall door.

"Gas?" one of the ambulance men says. "One of them geysers?" He shakes his head. "You're lucky he wasn't smoking cigarettes in there anyway!" He laughs. Paul's on the stretcher now, wrapped in a red blanket. They buckle a strap around him. "Who's coming with us?"

"Will he be all right?" I ask at last, in the ambulance.

"Ah yeah. We've got him on the oxygen now. He'll be grand in a few hours. A narrow escape though. It's a very common cause of death."

At the hospital the smog drifts into the corridors. They make me sit in a waiting room where there are plastic chairs, grey and red, around the walls, and in the middle two big ashtrays on stands, both overflowing. The floor is filthy. On the walls are signs saying SMOKE FREE ZONE, and diagrams of what tobacco does to your lungs. There is one other woman there, tiny and thin, with long blonde hair. She seems to be asleep. It's glamorous hair, silky and young, but she blinks and opens her eyes as my chair scrapes the floor and I see that her face is old, red and knobbly. She wears running shoes and faded denim jeans, a dirty red v-necked sweater and a chunky necklace. The knees of her jeans are soaked with blood, and one of her wrists is bandaged. She's very drunk.

"I didn't kill nobody," she says, swaggering in her chair and slurring the "nobody" like in a cowboy film. I'm afraid she'll fall off the chair, but she stares steadily at me. "They came for me first," she says.

I read all the posters, then I wander out into the hall, but when I try to go through the swing-doors to where Paul is, an ambulance man stops me. A nurse with a clipboard says I can see him in a few minutes, but not yet, not till the doctor finishes with him. She asks me his date of birth and his address. He's coming round, she says.

I go back to the waiting room. I sit on a red chair and run my finger over the cigarette burns on a grey one. The blonde woman is lying on the floor now, curled up on a spread-out newspaper. I think this time she's really asleep, but every so often she stirs and whimpers, or chuckles to herself. "Hold me," she murmurs, "Hold me."

When the nurse calls I follow her through the swing doors. Paul is confused, she tells me. He doesn't know where he is. He's wrapped in more red blankets and his eyes are closed, but when I take his hand he shouts "No!"

"Paul," I say, "it's all right. You're okay Paul." He looks at me and starts shouting again, "Leave me alone, Elaine, just fuck off and leave me alone!"

The nurse smiles at me, "It's a bit like waking up from an anaesthetic," she says, "but he'll be fine by tomorrow." She's apologising to me for his behaviour, but I'm the one who knows him, and I'm not Elaine. I think Elaine is the name of his brother's wife. The nurse is still talking: "The doctor says we'll be keeping him overnight, so you can go on home if you like. We're transferring him up to a ward now anyway."

As I stand at the phone in the smoggy corridor, trying to call a taxi, the blonde woman comes sleepily up and asks me for a cigarette. I tell her I'm sorry, I haven't any, but the ambulance man gives her his own, half-smoked. He rolls his eyes as she shuffles back in to sit down. "There was blue murder when we got there," he tells the nurse. He shakes his head and lights another cigarette, then paces up and down the hall again. In the waiting room the woman holds her cigarette between the fingers of her bandaged hand; holds that hand in the other, both hands between her knees. Her shiny blonde hair hangs down over them. She lifts her head and squints over at me, raising her chin to focus, "Are you a spy for the Big Boss?"

I try to grin without smiling. I won't bother you, please don't bother me. My taxi should come soon. I close my eyes and rest my forehead on one hand. The blonde woman begins to sing, and suddenly the sound of it rises up around my ears like a broken rainbow, finding and then losing the music, but rich and tuneful and full of sorrow. I hear her feeling around in her head and in the corners of the dirty room for the song, faltering at first and missing. At last she finds it and for two long slow lines she closes her eyes and raises her head again, and I see her shoulders and her face relax as she reaches up into the words: *He stripped her...and he ripped her... and...he cut her...in...three..., And he buried...her body... beneath a green... growing... tree.*

# BEAUTY TREATMENT

My Dad taught me how to do silly spelling, but I got into trouble for it at school the very next day. When I asked him how to spell "station," he winked at my mother and said "Station, nick a nation, fine fation, bobby ration, that's the way you spell station."

"Aw Dad," I said, "please!" but he just started to laugh and said "Please, nick a nease, fine fease, bobby rease, that's the way you spell please!"

"Dad!" I said, "I have to do my homework!" but all he said was "Homework, nick a nomework, fine fomework, bobby romework, that's the way you spell homework." He was laughing so much that I started to laugh too, in the end. "Silly," I said, "nick a nilly, fine filly, bobby rilly, that's the way you spell silly!" It turned out I knew how to spell "station" myself anyway, and we did a whole lot more words, with me doing my homework in between, until my mother said we were hopeless and she was going to bed.

When Miss Carty was correcting the copybooks, I taught Marian how to do it. First it was just ordinary words. People always talked in Miss Carty's class, but when she went to write something on the blackboard Marian whispered, "Carty, nick a narty, fine farty, bobby rarty," and I just exploded.

I knew she'd hear me, but the only thing I could do was take my hanky out of my sleeve and pretend I was blowing my nose. Miss Carty turned around.

"Una Fitzsimons and Marian Lacey," she said, "I am sick and tired. Sick and tired of you two."

The whole class was waiting to see how many slaps we'd get, but all she said was "Stand up when I'm talking to you!" Then when we stood up, the seat of our desk caught on the back of our legs. It went up with a crash, and someone started to laugh down at the back. Miss Carty was raging. Her voice always went squeaky and her face got red whenever people were messing at the back of the class, but it was her own fault. She always just stayed up near the blackboard. She never walked around or looked at people's copies or anything. I didn't look at Marian. I knew she'd be laughing. She could never keep a straight face, so I just kept swallowing down, trying to think of sad things.

"You'll wipe that smirk off your face, Marian Lacey," Miss Carty said, "when you're up here where I can keep an eye on you." She made Marian change places with a girl in the front row.

"Una Fitzsimons is a giddy fidget," she said to Marian, "but you're a bad influence." So Eilís Reynolds had to come and sit beside me.

I hated Miss Carty. I didn't even like her before she started picking on us. Marian hated her too, and on our way home we made up a story about her. How she got all the pimples on her face from rats sucking her blood, and how she had a boyfriend for a while but she never met him except when it was dark. She always wore a hat, then one night he said "Oh my darling, will you marry me?" but when he put his arms around her, her hat fell off, so he saw her horrible stringy black greasy hair and her pimply face, and he ran away. The reason she was so horrible was that her heart was broken.

It was no good sitting beside Eilís Reynolds. She wouldn't talk, or do anything. She was the slowest person in the whole class, always trying to finish writing things down off the blackboard. Even in the playground she always stayed near her big sister. They came to school together every day, and went home together, even though Eilís was old enough to go on her own, and her sister could have walked with her own friends.

The other teacher we had before Miss Carty was much kinder. She always said "Eilís Reynolds is a nice quiet girl," and let her clean the blackboard, or open the door. She never asked her any hard questions or made her read out loud. Miss Carty didn't even know Eilís was quiet. She used to keep giving her mental arithmetic sums to do, and spellings. Eilís was shaking every time she sat down after answering a question. She nearly always got them wrong.

Sometimes when Eilís was standing up trying to think of the answer, I'd pretend I was reading my book and try to give her a prompt, but she couldn't even hear me properly. I think it was because she was so frightened all the time.

One day my hand was on the seat in between us when she sat down. She grabbed hold of it and held on until she stopped shaking. So after that I used to just leave my hand on the seat any time Miss Carty asked her a question. She would hold on to it for a while, and she didn't shake so much. Miss Carty called her a dunce, though, and sometimes she'd ask me a question and I'd get it right, and then she'd say to Eilís, "I'm surprised some of Una Fitzsimons's brains don't rub off on you, sitting there," and everyone would laugh.

I was afraid to look at Eilís when Miss Carty said things like that, but she never seemed to notice. If I got everything right she used to even smile at me as though she was glad.

When we went out in our line to the toilets Miss Carty brought her cane, and anyone who was talking got slapped. One day though, no one was talking, but she was hitting people's legs with the cane anyway, for not walking in a straight line. She was shouting at everyone, and forgetting their names. When we came back to our classroom she started asking Eilís questions and she wouldn't stop. Eilís kept getting the answers wrong and in the end she started to cry. At last Miss Carty let her sit down and Eilís took out her hanky and blew her nose. Her hand was all wet and sticky when I took hold of it. I could still feel her shaking, but then Miss Carty said "I'm going to move you over where I can see you, Eilís Reynolds. You're getting away with murder down there." She made her change her place right over to the other side of the room, beside a new girl.

Miss Carty smiled at Eilís in her new place, and then back at me, a nasty smile. "Now we'll see how you get on without your protector!" she said to Eilís.

Miss Carty sat looking at us all for a minute, then she started talking about British Columbia. She was in a good humour again. She showed us British Columbia on the big map, then she took a magazine out of her bag and showed us the cover, with a picture of mountains and a lake with a boat on it.

"The climate of British Columbia is like Ireland," she said. "So if you're going to emigrate you should think about going there." She said a friend of hers was living there. He sent her the magazine. When she said "he," a couple of people sniggered and one girl said "Miss, would you like to emigrate to British Columbia?"

"That's enough," she said. "I want someone to read this out," and she looked around. I don't know why she picked on Eilís again. Eilís was hardly even able to read our ordinary English book, but she stood up in her new place and we were all waiting for her to read the magazine. I could see she was shaking. A few people were giggling and I heard somebody saying "A friend of mine...," imitating Miss Carty's country accent and her squeaky voice. Miss Carty glared around, but Eilís was still just standing there with the magazine in front of her on the desk.

The first thing that happened was Eilís giving a little cough, and then she just got sick, all down the front of her dress and all over the floor. Nobody said anything at all, not even Miss Carty. Everyone was just looking. Then we got a terrible fright when the bell rang for lunchtime. Miss Carty told the girl nearest the door to go and get Eilís's big sister to take her home, and the rest of us went out in our line the way we always did.

When we came back after lunch there was a big damp patch on the floor where Eilís got sick, and little bits of sawdust. Eilís didn't come back at all and I was in a desk by myself. The whole class was really quiet. Miss Carty gave us dictation

first, and then we had to read our books. When we got out at
four o'clock, I met Marian and walked as far as her bus-stop
with her. She was saying, "Her and her stupid old boyfriend
and her stupid old magazine." I said "I bet she never had any
boyfriend." I nearly said "I bet he'd get sick too," but I didn't
think of that till after Marian's bus came.

I walked on down to the main road by myself. I was looking
in the shop windows, and dragging my schoolbag along
because I didn't want to go home. My mother always told
people I loved school, but I didn't really, and I was afraid
she'd ask me about it. I looked in the shoemaker's window
for a while, at the little man with his hammer going up and
down, and the piles of old shoes on the shelf behind him. They
all had labels on them, but I couldn't read anyone's name. I
looked into the shop where they made you pay extra for
wafers with ice-cream, and then I came to the hairdressers'.

It was only a door between two shops, with a sign outside
that said MARJORIE, HAIR STYLIST. You had to go in
through the door and up the stairs. There was a perfume smell
and it was very dark until you got to the top. Upstairs the
perfume smell was stronger, but there was a big window, and
a whole lot of mirrors. I went up the stairs really just to see
what it was like, even though I'd been there before, when my
mother was getting her hair done. The women in there always
thought you were younger than you really were, but they were
very nice. They used to call you "pet" and "darling". They
had pink nylon overalls with sometimes sweets in their
pockets.

Marjorie came over to me. She was the boss. Her hair was
like candy floss, all silvery white and cloudy. I could see the
edges of her lipstick.

"Yes, Pet," she said, "what is it?" and I said "I want to make an appointment, please."

"For your Mammy, is it?" she asked.

"No," I said, "it's for another lady."

"What's the name, then?" She turned the big book around on the desk so she could see it.

"Miss Carty," I said.

"And what does she want done?"

"She wants a perm." I thought of something else, "and a blonde rinse."

Marjorie looked at me for a minute.

"Would tomorrow afternoon be all right? About half-four?"

I said yes. I said, "I'll tell her half-four," and I went out.


All the way home I was making up a picture in my head, like a picture in a comic. There was the main road, with all the shops on the two sides, but with no traffic, just people on the pavements, staring at the middle of the road. What they were staring at was a huge Miss Carty, lying on her back in the road. She stretched all the way from the traffic lights to down near our house, with her arms and her legs sticking out. Half her head still had the greasy black hair, but the other half was covered in bright yellow curls. She was going "Help! Help!" but nobody was helping her. Marjorie and a whole lot of other women were there in their pink overalls. They were all very small, but they had big pink lipstick smiles and they were dragging Miss Carty back into the hairdressers'.

# LE SOLEIL ET LE VENT

"In Benin, they were burning their forest—their tropical forest, you understand?  Hard trees: expensive wood. They were burning the forest, just to make salt."

We were a few miles from Le Pouliguen, walking towards the salt pans, and Annick was explaining them to me, talking slowly in a mixture of French and English so that I would understand.

"So people from here went...to Benin?"

Annick's chin went up and down as she nodded solemnly, "Ye-e-ess!"  Three syllables. Her hair was dry and shiny: a wiry gleam of grey mixed with dark brown that somehow told me she was a clean, kind woman without vanity. May in Kilderry had hair like that, I remembered suddenly. What was the trouble that time?  I didn't know any more, but May was kind. A stranger, not really an aunt, but I remembered the peace I felt at nine years old when she let me walk beside her for the cows and told me things about the trees, the animals, the neighbours' fields.

Hervé walked on the other side of me, watching Annick, watching my face to see if I had understood.

"*Oui*," he said now, smiling his neat smile, "*à Bénin—en Afrique*." He swept his arm out towards the sea, far.

"*Oui, oui!*" I nodded and smiled with more energy than I had felt in weeks. The effort of even such simple participation in another language seemed to require more oxygen. I was breathing deeper; using more of my body. I was like those children in the institute in Hungary whose brains can't move their limbs at first but then learn to: when enough kindness has been applied, and enough persistence.

"They went to Benin," I asked Annick, "to teach people?"

"Ye-e-ess," she said again, and gestured around at the honeycomb of land and water where we walked, now single file because the bank was narrow between the salt pans. Tufts of grass grew on either side of the foot-flattened clay; sun reflected off the water like slaps.

"They teach the people of Benin to do like this: *le soleil et le vent*. The sun and the wind: together they make salt. In Benin they boil the sea. They burn the trees—before. But in Brittany the people know for hundreds of years: *le soleil et le vent*."

"*Le soleil et le vent*," Hervé agreed, beaming, and we all three stood on the top of the sea wall, sun in our faces, wind in our hair, looking out over the Atlantic, calm and blue and heavy with salt. "Grind little mill, grind salt," I thought, and wondered how difficult it would be to tell them the story of the mill that churns out salt on the bottom of the sea. If I could remember it.

Behind us were the salt pans: hundreds of them, maybe thousands, lying in perfect flatness, rectangular, with rounded corners, moulded of clay and linked tortuously by channels that brought the sea in twice a day and trapped it there, making it give up its salt. In Ireland sometimes turf bogs are like that: flat and extensive; fragrant with the clean wind that blows across them, wild with plants and birds and insects, but cut in rectangles all the same, worked again and again by hands that have been respectful, yet insistent.

I was carrying a kilo of *gros sel* in my small backpack, and a half kilo of *fleur de sel*, together with a leaflet in four languages from the little wooden shop where we had left the car. All around us, scattered in the far and middle distance, people worked the basins. Once it was an occupation—a whole job—but now it is at best part-time. People have jobs in town, Annick told me. They come here when they can. Families own their own series of basins. Young men come on motor bikes to maintain the clay banks and harvest salt with the old wooden tools. I thought of the schoolteachers from Kerry who rent bogs in the Dublin mountains and go up there to cut their winter turf on summer evenings.

"*En Irlande*," I said, and they waited expectantly, but no more would come. I had to continue in English, "I have friends. *J'ai des amis*. I have friends who cut turf. You know turf? For the fire—not coal, not wood? Turf?"

"*Ah oui, ah oui*," Annick was nodding vehemently again, "*La tourbe. Oui, oui, on a vu, on a vu; les tourbières*." She appealed to Hervé, "*Tu te souviens? A Wicklow?*" Hervé remembered. He was a practical man. He noticed those things, and he acknowledged my attempt at communication by lighting his pipe and puffing happily.

I felt welcome. I walked behind Hervé in his brown cord trousers and his navy Breton sweater, catching the whiff of pipe smoke on the wind. Annick walked behind me; but at a crossway, the junction of four salt pans, I stood aside to let her pass, gesturing vaguely across the pattern of watery rectangles. I was trying to indicate a desire to gaze further; to scan the horizon for avocets, perhaps. They had mentioned avocets: wading birds with upcurved beaks. Amazing. I had never seen one, and I would have liked to, but I had developed these ways of turning my face away from people. Tears I couldn't control poured out of me so many times a day, it had become a habit. Mostly though, here among these orderly gardens of ocean, I felt the need to let a few beats go by in silence. I wanted somehow to wrap myself in the sudden safety I felt: this way of walking dry-shod above a flood; of being cocooned in warm uncomprehending kindness.

Annick and Hervé knew about Dónall. They had never met him—they'd only met me once before, after all—but they knew about the crash, and that he had died. And they knew we had no children. They knew my sister, and once, about seven years ago, when Dónall and I lived in Sandymount they had borrowed our house while we were away. They wrote in Christmas cards every year, "You must come to Le Pouliguen," and so I had.

I saw only men working as we walked back to the car, but the leaflet said that women worked here too, in the past anyway, especially on the *fleur de sel*. *Fleur de sel* is white, the way you would expect salt to be, but an hour here can teach you more about salt than would make sense anywhere else. *Gros sel* is brown and coarse, like crystallised porridge. They rake it off the bottom of the pans. There is so much of it, tied in bags with ribbons in every shop window—it's so mythologised—it's hard to realise it's not really food; that it's not good to eat in fistfuls. *Fleur de sel* is finer, more expensive: the first crystals that rise to the surface of the ponds as they evaporate, and in the past it belonged to women. They skimmed it from the surface of the water as it flowed curling and evaporating, shallower and shallower, brinier and brinier; and they sold it for money for themselves. In Ireland a woman could raise hens and sell the eggs. Of course there were fights. Mothers-in-law and daughters-in-law disputing control of the hens, and some of those disputes were vicious; but still an egg is a pleasant thing to contemplate, warm in a straw nest, carrying all that power and history.

*Fleur de sel* means "flower of salt". An effortless blossoming on the surface of the water. The name made me think of cotton sunbonnets: of women protecting their skin against that sun and wind. Already, after two hours, I could feel my own face hardening, my hands drying.


In the kitchen, on the shiny white board with its border of tomatoes, Annick wrote the word for the salt-pans. "Uh-yay," I had heard her say, but now she wrote, *oeillet*. Eyelet. Little eye. The local clay is watertight, so they can build banks and make basins that will contain the ocean, and each little salt-rimmed eye that gazes back at that blue sky is almost exactly ten by seven metres. It's all so simple, put like that.

"You are tired, Rosemary?" she said now. Hervé had already changed into wooden clogs and gone to work in his vegetable garden. We would not eat until eight.

Gratefully, I opened the narrow wooden door at the foot of the stairs and hauled myself up. There were three bedrooms here, under the roof, and a bathroom, and nobody but me to use them. Annick and Hervé had no children, but the house they had built for their retirement was big enough for visits from nephews and nieces and their children: their share of the French extended family at the seaside. I washed my face and tasted salt. I slathered moisturiser over my face and neck and went to my bedroom with its narrow white bed and dormer window. I had left the wooden shutters closed but now I opened them, leaning out over the sill to see the roofs and streets of the little town, and again that glittering sea beyond. There were two other beds in the room, pushed together under the sloping ceiling, and I began to order my possessions: to unpack all but underwear from my big soft bag and lay my tee-shirts in one neat pile; shorts in another; my dress and jeans side by side, draped quietly across one empty bed. I took the packets of salt from my backpack and placed them on the other bed, with the Maigret in French which I was probably never going to read, and the copy of *Jane Eyre* I'd bought at an exorbitant price in Paris.

I couldn't lie down. Neither of the books was what I wanted. I gathered up used tissues from under my pillow, from the pockets of my shorts, and from the floor. I found the plastic bag I'd used to carry a sandwich for the train and made it my *poubelle*: my wastebasket. Dog-eared bus tickets and months-old shopping lists went in there, and a scuffed-looking half-roll of Polo mints. And a little bunch of hair I dragged from my hairbrush. I took the crumpled Irish money from the pocket of my backpack and smoothed it, then made a pile of coins on top of it beside the salt. Next to the money I put my travellers' cheques and passport, then my keys from home and three small packets of tissues. My wallet was bulging with bits of paper: credit-card slips and French banknotes folded into neat rectangles, all with pinholes in the corners. I stood near the open window to do this part, breathing carefully as I removed everything. The credit card slips I glanced at one by one, then dumped. I counted the money. Enough for the next few days. The kidney-donor card made more tears come:

Dónall's signature was there as my next of kin. I dumped it too.

I knew the photograph was there, of course. I'd put it there myself. But I hadn't looked at it since the day after the funeral, when I'd found it in his wallet. The date was written on the back. March this year. The last time he went to New York to give lectures. And I recognised the woman: a graduate student who'd been at parties a year or two ago. Amy. Her hair was longer, and the child was in her arms, holding a strand of it. Clearly her child, and clearly also Dónall's: I'd seen enough of his own baby pictures not to be mistaken. A boy, a bit over a year old, probably.

Standing at the window, with the photo in my hand, I heard the high, sewing-machine whine of a Citröen 2CV, and a hum of other noises further away. Below me in the street there was laughter from people I couldn't see. I was very far away: from Dublin and from New York; from Dónall's colleagues and from mine, and all around me were French people on family holidays and the industrious sea, calmed and regulated, delivering its salt.

Suddenly I was too tired to do anything about the photo: to tear it up or burn it, or think of asking anyone about it. I was too tired to stand at the window even one more minute. I dragged the shutters closed and it was as though sleep entered the room: all I had to do was follow it to the bed and lie there, under the dark.

My feet shed sand as I pulled off my espadrilles, but I didn't care. I lay on the white candlewick bedspread until my bare legs felt cold, and then I pulled the edge of it up around me and lay some more. Up in that roof bedroom with the photo somewhere on the floor beside me, I floated above the landscape: the harsh, rocky, battered coast on one side of the peninsula and the neat, ruled accommodation of sea to land on the other. I saw women in cotton sunbonnets skimming the glittering salty flowers into baskets; saw them in silence, with their sleeves rolled up, their faces smiling. I saw the sea rolling in, twice a day, and I thought of the Irish words for tide, spring tide, sea-water: *taoille, rabharta, sáile*. I remembered the tidal rush of seaweed I ate once in Connemara, warm on brown bread, years ago, before I ever met Dónall. "*Goirt*," my mind said silently, the Irish word for salty. "*Is goirt iad na deora a shiltear*," they say, "*ach is goirte na deora nach siltear*." The tears that are shed are salty, but unshed tears are even saltier. Of course *goirt* means everything from salt to bitter.

Surely those women's hands were rough, with cuts and rips in the quicks of their fingernails; surely salt would sting? Of course it must, I told myself wearily, and felt my own tears yet again: not the small ones I knew before all this happened—the tears that are about something—but the big ocean of tears that lapped at my ankles all the time now and flowed right through me when it wanted to. I had learned by this time just to let it come—almost to admire it, the way I might the sea filling between rocks—but God I was tired of it.

I cried the way some babies cry: rhythmically, as though it were an exercise, lying with that white candlewick bedspread twisted around me, my face and the back of my hand smeared with salt and snot. Still my mind floated above, looking back along the railway I had travelled; following it beyond Paris, away to the east, through all those parts of eastern Europe where I had never been, but maybe I could go now. I thought of rooftops, and of rooms beneath them, and of all the books written about the people in those rooms.

"It's only a woman crying in a bedroom," my mind said to me then, surprising me. "A well-known literary trope. You're in good company. You're quite safe. You have a bedroom in which to cry."

I could see chinks of light around the edges of the shutters, and hear more voices, muffled, from the street. The room was full of quiet shapes: a bluish darkness where I could see quite clearly, and my eyes travelled around, counting everything. I started to unwind the bedspread. I had a full hour until I should offer to help with dinner, and soon I was going to walk across the wooden floor to the empty bed, where I would get a tissue and blow my nose. Then I would open the blue ribbon on the white cotton bag of *fleur de sel*, moisten my finger and dip it in. I wanted to taste one perfect salt crystal on my tongue.

# THE BACK WAY HOME

There was one day Eugene didn't come home from school.
He was supposed to walk home by himself in the evening
because he got out half-an-hour before me. He'd walk all the
way down on the other side of the main road, then get Miss
Fay to cross him. I had to do it myself when I was small. Miss
Fay's was across from the bottom of our road. You had to go
into the shop and just look at the biscuits in the tins with the
glass tops till she was ready. Then she'd lift up part of the
counter and come out in her white coat. She'd wait till there
were no cars coming, then we'd both walk right out into the
middle of the road. I'd run across the rest of the way and she'd
go back to the shop.

There were cars and buses and lorries on the main road,
but we often saw whole flocks of sheep as well, with men
walking behind, shouting at them, and sometimes there were
big splashed cow-plops all down the middle of the road when
we were crossing.

I always came in the back way, up the lane, so I could see
if anyone was out playing. Our houses were all joined together
and usually only grown-ups or boys were out on the road.

Girls played in the back lane, but this day there wasn't anyone. Our gate was never bolted except at night, so I only had to lift the latch and go in.

The twins' toys were all over the grass when I opened the gate, but no one was there, and the back door was closed. When I opened it the draught made the kitchen door bang. That meant the front door was open, so I dropped my schoolbag and went to look. I thought maybe there was a visitor, a long-lost friend of my parents who would tell me about the time before I was born. But there wasn't any visitor, just my mother at the door looking out. She came back in.

"Eugene isn't home, Una. Did you see him on your way?"

"No," I said. We were always being warned about getting lost but I couldn't believe Eugene really was. I was a bit jealous.

"I'll have to go out," my mother said. "You'll have to stay here with James and John."

"Aw do I have to?" I said, but she wasn't even looking at me. She was taking off her apron, putting on her coat, and her face was all red. I thought I'd better not say anything. The twins were playing on the floor. I sat down at the table, looking out the window.

I didn't know where Eugene could be. There were supposed to be people who took children away but I didn't really believe in them. If someone stopped in a car and offered you sweets you had to say No Thank You, and run away, but I'd never heard of it happening to anyone.

I wasn't there very long. I heard the front door again, and my mother's voice saying to someone "Thank you very much. He's very silly. You were very good, thank you." Eugene came in and she came after him with her hair all tossed, taking off her coat.

"Where were you?" I said to Eugene in a cross voice. He didn't seem a bit sorry.

"A man brought me home," he said. He was smiling, but his face was all streaky and his glasses were smeared. He must have been crying.

"What man?" I asked.

"A man found him up outside the Post Office," my mother said, "crying. He said he couldn't find the way home, so the man brought him."

I thought that was ridiculous.

"What were you doing up outside the Post Office? That's not the way home!"

"I was trying to find the other way," Eugene said, "The way we come from the swings."

"Don't be so stupid," I said. I was really annoyed. It would be miles to walk around by the park if you were coming from school. He was just looking for notice.

"Leave him alone, Una," my mother said. "He got a bad fright." But she didn't give out to me for saying stupid. She went into the scullery and got out a whole packet of marshmallow biscuits, the kind with raspberry jam down the middle. She put the kettle on and gave Eugene milk in a mug. She broke a rusk in half for the twins. Then she made tea for herself and me, and the three of us sat at the table.

"What kind of a fright?" I asked. I was getting a bit frightened myself. Eugene was taking the rows of marshmallow off the biscuits and sucking the coconut off them. He was holding them up like big shiny pink worms and Mam wasn't saying anything to him.

"They said they'd take me to the slaughterhouse."

"Who'd take you to the slaughterhouse?"

"The men up on the main road outside Mooney's."

Mam didn't know what he was talking about, but I did. The men were digging a hole in the road. We used to cover our ears going past when they were drilling, but the sound came up out of the ground right through your legs. They had a sort of a canvas tent that they sat inside, on boxes, drinking tea, and a fire in a thing like a big bucket with legs, with all holes in the sides. There was no smoke like with coal. It was coke. If you looked across the top of it at anything, it went all wobbly and wavy.

The men used to shout at anyone who went too near the fire or the hole, but I didn't think they'd take anyone to a slaughterhouse.

"I bet the men never said that," I said to Eugene.

"Not the men," he said. "The men didn't say it. It was Doreen Casey and her friend."

I knew who Doreen Casey was, and my mother knew as well. We bought all our meat in Casey's shop. Doreen was in the class below me but she always had really grown-up clothes. Anyone whose father was a butcher always had nice clothes. Mary Morgan in my class: her father was a butcher too, and their sitting room was upstairs because the shop was downstairs. She had lovely clothes and hair that was nearly to her waist and sometimes I walked part of the way home from school with her. I liked her, but I didn't like Doreen Casey.

Eugene stopped messing with the biscuits and told us what happened.

He was walking home with his schoolbag when he saw Doreen Casey and her friend at the bus-stop near Mooney's and they called him to come over. So he went over to them and said "What?" and they said "Do you see those men down there? Do you know what they're doing?" And he said "What?" and they said "They're waiting for boys with glasses. They're going to take them away."

He was a bit frightened. "No they're not," he said.

"Oh yes they are!" they said. "They take them to the slaughterhouse and cut them up."

They kept on laughing at him and telling him he'd better watch out, talking about the slaughterhouse till he thought he'd better go another way home, and that's how he got lost.

"That's a lot of nonsense," my mother said. "You shouldn't listen to that sort of talk. You should have more sense. Of course those men wouldn't take you to a slaughterhouse."

"Is there really a slaughterhouse?" Eugene asked.

My mother was going into the scullery with the cups. "No, of course not," she said. "Those men are fixing the road. They're not interested in cutting up little boys. Nobody cuts up little boys."

But the thing is, I knew there really was a slaughterhouse. It was in the lane behind Mary Morgan's father's shop. She let me look in through the gate at it on our way home from school, and now I felt sick thinking about it, all the dirt and the blood.

I liked walking home with Mary Morgan. She had lovely long blonde hair and clean clothes every day. Everyone wanted to be friends with her. Then one day she said "Do you want to see the slaughterhouse?" I didn't know what that was, but I said yes.

It was the first time I was ever up her back lane. It wasn't like ours. You could go all the way along it and out the other end, and there was no grass or nettles, just concrete with high walls on the two sides, and an echo. It was too narrow for people to play, so we didn't see anyone.

I walked along behind Mary Morgan in her lovely pink dress till she came to a big sort of gate, like a garage door. The paint was all bubbles and flaky, and in some places you could see the wood. I could hear something that sounded like cows. Mary Morgan whispered to me to come up beside her. She was looking in at the yard through a crack, and there was a cow in there. Mary Morgan's father was there, and her uncle. I knew them from passing by their shop going to school. I hoped they wouldn't look over and see my eye at the crack.

There was another man in there as well. Three men, all wearing wellingtons and skidding around, and the ground was covered with cow dirt and blood. There were an awful lot of flies, and a smell that made me feel sick. Mary's father and the other man had two ropes around the cow's neck. They were pulling as hard as they could, but the cow was trying not to come out of the shed. It was brown and white, with curly hair on its head, and making a horrible sound. It wasn't very tall.

It came out of the shed slowly, leaning backwards, and then Mary's uncle just walked up right in front of it. He had a gun in his hand, only very short and square-looking, not shiny. He held it right in the cow's forehead and that was all. It wasn't even really like a bang, but the cow shivered all over and then the feet skidded out from under it. Mary's uncle jumped out of the way, and the cow fell down in the muck, on top of its own legs.

Mary Morgan whispered in my ear "Do you want to go home now?"

I nodded my head and we ran all the way to the end of the lane. When we came out on the main road I saw all the people walking around, and Mary Morgan went up one way to her house and I went the other way to mine. I walked all the way up our road to the front door that day, instead of around the back.

Mary Morgan told me they always slaughtered on Tuesdays, and I could come and look some other time if I wanted. I said I would, but the next time I passed their shop I saw her uncle out in front of the counter where the floor was covered with sawdust. He had wellingtons on and there were marks of blood all over his white apron.

"Where are you going, Una?" Mam said. "Dad'll be home soon. It's time to set the table."

"The toilet," I told her. I had to think of a way to warn Eugene about the slaughterhouse without getting everybody frightened again.

# HAM

When Eileen first went to America she couldn't get over how many fat people there were, or how far it was to the shops. She wrote me the funniest letters. There was something about the way they measure things in blocks. All the streets in the first place she went to were dead straight, and there was exactly the same distance between side roads, but of course she didn't know that at the beginning. One evening she went out for cigarettes and a bottle of milk, and someone told her it was about twelve blocks, but all she could think of were the little wooden blocks Declan played with—Ciaran wasn't born yet—so she ended up walking miles! The temperature was way over ninety and people couldn't believe she'd *walked* to the market.

That was another thing. They called it a market, but it turned out to be a huge modern supermarket. More like an aeroplane hangar, she said, out in the middle of nowhere, and there were three pages of description of all the things on the shelves. I used to sit reading her letters at the kitchen table with tears running down my face laughing. I could just see the rows and rows of dog food, and Eileen trying to make the black women at the checkouts understand her accent.

Then when she finally came home, she was amazed at how small the paper towels were, and the milk cartons, and the fridge. She kept noticing things that were smaller, making little tiny shapes with her hands, and laughing. I thought to myself the first day, Oh God, don't tell me she's turned into another one of these Yanks! But I didn't say anything, and I'm glad now I didn't. I couldn't anyway, could I? With the funeral, and trying to cope with the kids, and Brian, and all his mother's old neighbours wanting to drop in and talk about her. She was Eileen's mother too, though God forgive me I never could stand the woman. Still, she's gone, and she won't bother me any more, and the least I could do was look after the mourners.

It suited me to go to Shannon for Eileen. It got me out of the house and away from the cooked ham and the sliced bread for the best part of a day. Her plane was getting in at some ungodly hour, and you wouldn't wish it on your worst enemy to make their way up here by bus after that. I wouldn't let the boys come either. She was my friend before she was their auntie, I told them, and I thought I deserved that much. I wondered if nine years would have changed her. At school she was the one who made my life bearable. I remembered her making us all laugh in the dormitory, clowning around, then brushing her hair like mad before lights out. I thought about her at our wedding, in her blue dress and straw hat, with one long dark plait down her back, and I knew I'd never feel like a hypocrite with her. Nine years was a long time though.

Driving down through Mayo and Galway was lovely, with the sun coming up and mist clearing off the fields, and I thought back to the time it took Eileen and me a week to hitch-hike to Kerry by the back roads. Every lift was about four or five miles, and they all ended at creameries or pubs, or gates into fields. We walked a lot of the way, past fuchsia hedges and black-and-white cows, from where one car let us off to where another picked us up. I always sat in the saggy leather back seats while Eileen sat up in front and chatted away. She always seemed to know someone they knew, or they knew her uncles, or her brothers. It was one of the great things about not being from Dublin, I thought. If you lived in the country, you were at home anywhere, or maybe it was having brothers.

If it wasn't for Eileen I never would have married Brian. I wouldn't even have met him. And then where would I be? I fell in love with the whole family, I suppose. I just wanted a piece of their life. It wasn't that he even looked like her, but there was something about their voices. All the Lallys speak the same way. Of course that was before I discovered what the mother was like. You don't notice those things when you're sixteen, especially if the alternative is slouching around the red-brick roads at home, waiting for the summer to end — or the sky to fall.

Eileen was one of the last to come off the plane, but I knew her the second I saw her. Her hair was cut very short, and she wore long dangly earrings, but the face was just the same. Maybe a bit thinner. She always used to say she couldn't get a tan, but she certainly had one now. She came rushing up, laughing, to give me a hug, and the walk was the same as well. Something about her shoulders always looks full of energy, and remember this was after a six-hour flight from New York, and God knows how long before that.

"Liz, you're exactly the same, it's fantastic to see you!" Her voice didn't even sound American. Her accent was still the same as Brian's, but I'd forgotten how much more musical her voice was. When she let go of me she bit her lip suddenly. Her face loosened and her eyes got wet, "How are they all at home?"

I was embarrassed then. Here was I so glad to see her, and the only reason she was here was her mother was dead.

"Oh they're OK, you know. I don't think it's really sunk in yet. They're going to be delighted to see you anyway."

Walking to the car she kept stopping to sniff the air. "You've no idea how good it is to be back. I was bawling crying on the plane coming in, and the woman beside me thought it was for Mammy—I told her I was coming home for the funeral—but it wasn't. Does that sound terrible?"

"What were you crying for?"

"It was something about the fields. They were so green and small, and all different shapes."

I started to laugh, but Eileen wasn't joking. "You've no idea what it's like, Liz, flying over the Midwest. They haven't had rain there for months and it's all just brown. The corn all withered in the fields. Mile after mile. It goes on forever, huge brown squares and brown rectangles. Then you get to the ocean, and after that it's just ocean, and it was dark anyway."

"You should be working for Bord Fáilte. Little Green Emerald Isle, is that it?"

She laughed. "No I shouldn't, but I see what they mean. You're above the clouds when the sun comes up, and suddenly they tear apart, and it looks so *gentle* down there. And then the coast. Oh God I could nearly taste the salt when I saw all those little tails and trails of land stretching out into the sea. When all this is over I don't care what anyone says, I'll have to get off by myself for a few good walks."

As I started the car I was hoping she would get her walks. I wasn't too hopeful, considering what Brian had said about his mother's will. That's if it was a proper will. Eileen would have her work cut out for her with the solicitors and the insurance company. Two weeks, she'd told Brian on the phone. That wouldn't be very long.

We drove up through Clare, talking about everything, laughing a lot of the time. Eileen said she was tired, but she didn't sound it. She knew I hadn't had an easy time with her mother, but she didn't make any fuss about it: some of the time she talked about her, and a few times she cried a bit, but mostly she talked about other things—things we both remembered.

We stopped for lunch in Galway. Eileen spotted the place before I did, and it was lovely: homemade vegetable soup in big deep pottery bowls, and three different kinds of cheese with brown bread. There were paintings for sale on the walls, and the sun came in the door and lay across our feet as we ate. I could see Eileen better, now I wasn't driving, and she was a lot thinner than I remembered. I used to be the thin one. She was wearing a long, loose, purple shirt over a white teeshirt, and her wrists looked narrow and elegant in the sleeves. It's not a colour I would ever have thought of buying, but it suited her, especially in that place. It took ten years off me, sitting there with her, and I wouldn't even have been surprised to see our two old canvas rucksacks lying against the wall.

Getting back into the car I remembered again that we were grown up now, and on our way to a funeral. Eileen smiled sadly at me, "I suppose it'll be all cups of tea and ham sandwiches from here on in." At the same moment we both remembered one of those farmers who gave us a lift years ago, a real joker. He said he was coming from a funeral, and that he'd never seen such a big one. "Big funeral, did you say?" Eileen said now, imitating him. She screwed up her face, "Sure didn't the widow have two men out behind the house stripped to the waist, mixing mustard for the sangwiches!" We laughed for a long time at that, but the rest of the journey was quiet. Eileen dozed a bit, and cried a bit, and looked out the window a bit, and I wondered when we'd have a chance to talk to each other in peace again.

It started to rain just after we got to Sligo, and it didn't stop for days, but we got through the funeral all right. There seemed to be hundreds of people coming and going from the house, but we kept making sandwiches, and some of the neighbours brought apple tarts, and Brian kept carrying crates of empty Guinness bottles through the kitchen to stack them outside the back door. It turned out Eileen didn't eat meat, but she was very good about it. She looked after herself somehow.

When it was all over, she bought an umbrella and borrowed an old fawn raincoat of mine, and every day one of us drove her into Sligo. The sky was damp and dark, and the pavements never dried out, but she went splashing off through the puddles to deal with all the business that had to be cleared up. I felt sorry for her. She was cold all the time, and she seemed to have faded since she got here. She hadn't worn earrings since the first day, and she never wore lipstick, so now her short hair made her look small and a bit pathetic. But then she'd say something that really got on my nerves. This house may not be what she's used to, but it's certainly not damp. Or the business about how small everything was again. Sligo, for instance—I know it's not a big city, but she grew up there, for God's sake, and now she says everything seems so narrow, and so close together that she's afraid the buildings are going to fall over on top of her! When she said things like that I felt like telling her to just shut up. Or reminding her she was staying in my house and wearing my clothes. But then she was so great with the kids. She's the only auntie they have. And when it comes down to it, she was great with me too. She could still make me laugh like no one else, and she used to hug me. Nobody except the kids has given me a hug for years, but Eileen said everyone hugs their friends in Madison, Wisconsin.

On the second Thursday she asked if I'd help her go through her mother's stuff. She only had four days left, and all the clothes were still in the wardrobe in the house. The dressing-table drawers were full, and then there were the chocolate boxes: boxes and boxes of old Christmas cards under the stairs and God knows what in the way of broken rosary beads and holy pictures on the high shelves. It's not the kind of thing I enjoy, but it gave me an excuse to send the kids off with Brian, and I didn't know when I'd have a good chat with Eileen again.

The first thing she said after we climbed the stairs in her mother's house surprised me so much I had to sit down.

"I'm thinking of staying on, Liz," she said. I sat on the padded yellow dressing-table stool and looked at her. I don't know why I was so amazed. This is her country after all.

"The shop comes to me, you know."

I nodded. Of course she'd sell it, but what would she get for a dusty old shop full of corsets and white baby clothes?

"Do you remember the place we stopped in Galway?"

"Of course."

"I could set up a place like that. There isn't one in Sligo, but I know how to run one."

I hadn't seen her grin like that since the day she arrived.

"The Co-op in Madison is that kind of place and I've been more or less running it for years. I haven't decided anything yet, but I spoke to Tim Wilson about the idea and he didn't think there'd be any problem with the legal end." She was so excited that her shoulders were going again. Her hands were fluttering as she described where she would put a food counter, and how the tables would be laid out, and what the colours would be, and looking at her sitting there on the edge of her mother's bed, as she made plans for me as well as for herself, I imagined I could see the long plait hanging over her shoulder again.

"I was even thinking we could whitewash the yard at the back. It'd be lovely in the summer with a whole lot of geraniums and a few tables out there too." That part made me laugh, and I interrupted her,

"In the rain?"

"It doesn't rain all the time. It's even clearing up now. Look!"

We both walked to the window, and sure enough, we could see all the way over to Knocknarea to a patch of high clean dry blue sky.

"But do you think you could settle down here? Would you not miss America?"

"I would of course, but I miss here when I'm there. I'd miss you, and I'd miss the kids, especially now I've just got to know them." She put one arm around my shoulders and hugged me. "And there are things here you don't get anywhere else. People have time to talk to you. It's never too hot, and you never have three feet of snow outside the door. And then you have the sea."

"You never got your walks," I said.

"I will tomorrow though," she said, with another happy grin. "Tim Wilson has to go out to Raughly to see someone, and he said I can come along if it's fine and walk for as long as I like."

I followed her down the stairs, getting used to the idea that she might be around for years. That we could take up where we left off. With the kids in school I could help her a lot with the shop, and maybe I could cook all the stuff Brian won't eat. Meals without meat. Things with garlic in them. Maybe she'd come with me to Dublin some time, and I could buy a few clothes. I was glad Tim Wilson was being nice to her. I never cared for him myself, with his thick neck and his fat hands, his good suits and his white shirts, and his little thin frightened wife. But that's the thing about Eileen. She's much more open to people than I ever was. She can get through to them and make you see the good in them.

The weather cleared up by teatime, and Friday was like a miracle, dry and sunny. I envied Eileen going off to Raughly, even if it was with Tim Wilson. She was wearing her own clothes: white jeans and a soft blue shirt, and she'd put in her long silver earrings again. It was funny to see her sitting into the BMW beside big pink Tim. Raughly is a place I used to love going, but I haven't had a walk there since before the boys were born. It's wild and sandy and windy, and I imagined Eileen walking away from the car, out to where the road gets softer and sweeter underfoot as the paving gives way to grass and sand, and then sitting in her blue shirt on the edge of the stone pier, looking out over the sea.

I opened all the windows to let the lovely warm breeze blow into the house, and then I took a notion to take down the curtains and wash them. All the cigarettes people smoked during the funeral! That was another thing Eileen complained about. I never did smoke myself, but I know there's nobody worse than a reformed smoker for fussing about it. It was nice to get the curtains out on the line though. My mother-in-law was dead and buried, and now the last bits of her ghost were blowing away in the wind. It was just as well neither Brian nor Eileen was there to see me doing my little dance! Declan was in the garden next door, and I saw him looking up at me, but Ciaran didn't take any notice, just kept on building his fort until I called them for their lunch.

When they went out again to play I put on the kettle to make myself a cup of tea. There was some cooked ham left in the fridge, but I couldn't look at it. I took down the big cookery book Eileen sent me years ago, and then I cut up a couple of tomatoes and ate them with bread while I read about blueberry pancakes and spinach quiche, pumpkin bread, and casseroles made of walnuts and lentils, or broccoli with mushrooms and sour cream.

I was still reading when I heard Tim's car on the gravel.
The front door was open, and as I walked out into the hall, I
saw Eileen get out and walk up the drive without even closing
the car door behind her. I stood waiting for Tim to get out, or
wave, but he just slammed the door from the inside and turned
the car fast in the gateway. Eileen marched past me into the
kitchen, red in the face, waving her arms. I closed the front
door as quietly as I could and followed her in.

"Jesus!" she said, almost shouting, "I don't believe that
asshole!" Suddenly she'd turned into an angry American
stranger, storming into the middle of my kitchen and yelling
at me, and I didn't know what to say. Then I noticed a dirty
black streak across the knees of her jeans, and I saw that one
of her earrings was missing.

"What happened?"

"That guy is just a joke, do you know that? Do you know
what he did? He drove down this quiet little road to one of
those abandoned piers, and then he tried to climb on top of
me!"

"Oh God," I said, "was he serious?"

"Dead serious. He tried to rape me. I couldn't believe the
things he was saying to me. I mean give me a break! His wife
doesn't understand him, he says, and he knows I'm a liberated
woman. Christ! And he bets I know a trick or two—Jesus,
such *crap*!"

I closed the back door and the kitchen window. She was
really shouting, but at least she sat down.

"What did you do?"

"I took this out of my pocket." It was a little red penknife,
"and I told him that if he so much as laid a finger on me again
I would cut his balls off and hang them around his neck!"

Suddenly she burst out laughing. "Oh Liz, you should have seen the look on his face."

I could imagine it only too well, and I felt sick in my stomach thinking about it. She went on talking about Raughly, and the weather, and what Tim said first, and what he said then. She told me about her self-defence class, and sexual harassment, and consciousness-raising, and legislation. I made another pot of tea and we drank it together, but I really couldn't concentrate. She should have known what to expect, or I should have known, and warned her. I don't know what I was thinking of to let her go off on her own like that with a married man. And then to threaten him! Maybe that kind of language is all right in Madison, Wisconsin, but you really can't talk like that to people here, especially not people like Tim Wilson. I kept thinking about all the committees and things he's on, and the ways he could get back at us.

That was yesterday. She hasn't mentioned her restaurant plan since, and I think it's just as well. It was lucky I was on my own in the house when she got back, so she got it out of her system before Brian and the boys were around. I hope she understands to keep her mouth shut in front of Brian. She's upstairs packing now. I've asked her to come to the pictures with me tonight, and if I organise a picnic tomorrow with the kids, with any luck nothing else will happen before she gets on that plane on Monday.

# CHARM

When I was eleven I started to grow very tall, and people said things like "We'll have to put a brick on top of her head." A doctor and a nurse came to the school to examine us and gave me a note to take home. "Looks anaemic," it said. My mother ordered Jersey milk from the milkman and I had to drink a whole bottle every day.

One time when I came into the kitchen my mother and father were talking. They told me I was going to Templegarve for the summer.

"And we'll have no long faces, please," my father said. "You spend too much time out in that back lane. A bit of fresh air will do you good."

Maybe he thought I really liked the back lane. I was always out there in the summer, but it was only because there was nowhere else to go. I was dying to go down the country. I knew there'd be all different places I could explore. I'd be the youngest instead of the eldest so I wouldn't get into so much trouble, and there'd be animals.

I was never in Templegarve before. It was the place where my mother grew up, but any time we asked about going there my father laughed and said "Oh my God! What would you want to go there for? Sure it's the back of beyond." My mother only said it was too far. There were too many of us and it wouldn't be fair to Auntie Tess.

The first day when I woke up there I didn't know where I was—I could hear men's voices right beside my head outside the window, and the sloshy sound of their feet with wellingtons on, and buckets clanking. It was so late when we got there in the night that I didn't see anything, and I was so tired I didn't even notice I was sleeping downstairs. My Dad was with me—sleeping in the other bed—but he said he had to leave straight after breakfast to go and see a man. I went out and waved.

"Come on, Una," Auntie Tess said, "we'll go and get the eggs."

I wondered where all my cousins were, but she didn't say anything about them. I went with her to the barn. There was a row of wooden boxes with straw in them and some had an egg in them and some had none, and when Auntie Tess saw all the empty boxes she made little disgusted sounds with her tongue and said "That old black hen's laying out again."

Every day after that I went by myself to look for eggs: in the barn and in the little shed, and sometimes in the ditch beside the garden. I found out where my cousins were too. Robert was married and Gerry was in Canada, so only Michael and Teresa were at home. Teresa was nearly thirteen. She was the one I already knew. I thought we'd be sleeping in the same room, but I had Gerry's room instead—the one who was in Canada—in the old part of the house. I had a nightlight like a little candle, a washstand with a jug and a basin, a potty under the bed because it was so far to the bathroom, and a rug made out of rags because the floor was concrete under the lino. Teresa's room had a blue carpet, a blue bedspread and blue curtains. She never got up before ten o'clock.

Teresa didn't ever want to play with me. Once when I asked her to come and play in the hay she said "I'm too old to play stupid eejit baby games!" but I didn't care. I thought she was the stupid eejit, staying in all the time. A lot of days I went over to Molloys on the other side of the main road to see Brian. He was only nine but he called all the grown-up people by their first names and he said he knew how to drive the tractor, only his father wouldn't let him. We went all around our yard and his yard, looking into all the sheds, and sometimes up around the land and into other people's land as well. He showed me where the bull was, but he said "You better not ever let on you saw it or I'll get leathered for bringing you here." He said he often went right up to the bull, but he wouldn't do it while I was there.

Bernie was at Molloys as well. She was their cousin and she had a job in the hospital for the summer. She was from another place up in the mountains, called Derrylynch, that Brian said was the arse-end of nowhere. He was always teasing her, saying things like that. Any time Bernie didn't like something she said it was cat, and Brian used to go around after her asking her if the dog was cat. He said cat himself though, and if he was talking about something really bad, like his school, he said it was cat melodeon. When Bernie bought a skirt to wear for her interview for nursing he said it was duckshit green. She chased him out of her room, but she let me stay.

Bernie had a dressing table all covered in make-up things, and a whole lot of necklaces and different scarves hanging beside the mirror. She showed me how to try on her make-up and she said when she was a nurse she'd probably marry a doctor and I could come and visit her in her big house. She was always talking about what dance she was going to, and sometimes when I was there she took off her clothes and tried on other clothes and asked me if they suited her. She put talcum powder in her shoes and in the inside of her clothes under the arms. She asked me "Does your mother use deodorant?" but I didn't know. She told me about all the dances and who got off with who, and about getting a lift home with someone one night. She wouldn't tell me who, but she said it was cat, the things some of them expected. She was giggling, but then she stopped, "Now mind you, I'm very particular. Don't you go saying things to your Auntie, giving her the wrong idea."

I said I wouldn't say anything.

"You wouldn't, would you?" She started to smile again. "I'll tell you who I wouldn't mind getting a lift from though—our Mister Brown Eyes!" and she started to tickle me.

Bernie often said things I didn't really understand and then went on talking about something else. I didn't mind much: I liked going into her room and she didn't treat me like a baby. The only thing I didn't like was when she tickled me or poked me in the chest and said "Your turn will come too." Or "Wait till you fill out a bit and start going to dances—you'll be mad after the fellas yourself in a few years."

If she saw Brian and me going off out the fields together she always said "Oh-oh, the young lovers!" or "Wait till I tell your Ma!" but Brian said to me "Don't mind that one, she's only an old sex maniac. She's as thick as two short planks."

The person I liked talking to the best was Michael. He was twenty and very tall, with black hair. He was always smiling. He went to the creamery every morning with four big churns of milk in the trailer behind the car, and he came back with the four churns full of skim milk. I started to get up earlier and earlier so I could watch him milking. All the different cats used to come and drink some of the milk off old saucers. There were about ten of them and only some of them had names. Whitey was an old one that had lost an eye in a fight and he could only turn around one way, so if the milk was on the other side of him he had to walk all around in a circle to get to it. Michael said he probably only had four-and-a-half lives left. He wouldn't let me pet any of them.

"They're wild, them cats." he said. "You want to watch them. They'd scratch you as quick as look at you."

"Why are they here if they're wild?"

"They work for a living, the same as the rest of us," he said. "If you didn't have cats on a farm, you'd have mice all over the place, and rats."

"Did you ever see a rat?" I asked him. He laughed.

"Did I ever what?" he said. "Sure they're everywhere. But they mind their manners wherever there's cats."

I talked to Michael all the time he was getting ready to go to the creamery. Some days he let me come with him and I stood out of the way, watching all the farmers and the men in the white coats who took the milk in. On the way home he always stopped to buy the newspaper and a few times he bought me a comic. They were the same comics as the ones at home, with girls wanting to be ballet dancers, and running away from orphanages to find their real parents, but they seemed to be different when I read them in Michael's car with all the dust, and the bits of straw, and my own knees always dirty. Once we saw a dead cat on the road and I felt sick, but Michael made me laugh. He said "Would you look at that: nine lives gone. If it was a dog it'd be only one!" A few minutes after that we saw three cats alive outside a house and I said "There's twenty-seven lives." Michael laughed when I said that. He said "That's my girl, Una! You're all there, aren't you?"

One evening after tea, he asked me if I wanted to go and look for rabbits. I nearly couldn't believe it, but I knew we were really going when Auntie Tess told me to go and get my jersey. Before we went out the door Michael reached up over the mantelpiece and took down a gun. He put it behind us on the back seat and told me not to touch it. The car went much faster without the trailer behind and we went bumping and flying over the potholes all the way to the main road, then we turned towards the west, in the direction away from the creamery.

One of the things I didn't know about Templegarve before I went there was that it was only six miles from the sea. We had to walk up from the beach across the rocks to get to where the rabbits were, and Michael showed me how to put sand on the soles of my shoes so I wouldn't slip. I was never on a beach so late before, and the sand was cold. The sun was going down out over the sea and we could see it shining all red between the gaps in the stone walls. Michael was carrying the gun. I didn't want to ask him what it was for. I just walked very quietly along behind him, trying not to make a sound even when we were getting over walls and some rocks tumbled down. We came to one wall and Michael flapped his hand to tell me to get down. I nearly laughed. It was like Cowboys and Indians, only with a real gun. We peeped up over the wall and there were all the little rabbits in a field at evening, like our poem at school. They were just nibbling all over the field, all their little white tails, but then the gun went off right beside me and the rabbits raced away like the way water splashes when you throw a rock in.

I got a terrible fright. I looked at Michael to see if he was hurt but he was standing up looking out at the empty field, saying "Shit!"

"What's the matter?" I said, "Why did it go off?"

"I told you to keep your head down," he said. "Are you thick, or what?" He told me to stay where I was, then stepped over the wall and walked out into the field with the gun hanging down under his arm. I sat on the ground, shivering a bit and crying a bit, looking out at the sea. It was all red and everything was quiet. When he came back he was carrying a dead rabbit hanging down by its legs. He was smiling.

"Aw Una," he said, when he saw I was crying, "Come on, don't be a baby, I was only teasing you. We had good hunting, didn't we? That's my girl."

I stood up and we started back down to the beach.

"You'll never make a farmer's wife if you can't stand killing things," Michael said, but he let me walk on the other side of him so I didn't have to be beside the rabbit.

"We'll watch the sun go down on Galway Bay," he said, "Did you ever hear that song? Over there's where Gerry is. Canada."

"Is he younger than you?" I asked. I knew he was, because Bernie told me he was in the same class as her at the Tech, but I wanted Michael to keep talking.

"Three years younger," Michael said, "Seventeen. He only left school this year, but my mother's brother asked him out there, to see if he'd like it."

"Were you ever in Canada?" I asked him.

"No," he said, "but I'll tell you one thing, as soon as that fellow gets back, I'll be off."

"Where will you be off to—Canada as well?"

"Oh, I don't know. Anywhere. I'll have to see a bit of the world. I only have the one life and I'm damned if I'm going to spend it lugging milk churns around."

I felt terribly sad that he might go away.

"Will you ever come back?" I asked him.

"Oh I suppose so," he said. "A few years away would do me."

I felt better. I was thinking about books where the man says to the girl "I have to go away, but will you wait?" Michael wouldn't say anything like that probably, but I'd wait for him anyway. I'd have to go to school till I was about seventeen, but after that I could spend my life collecting the eggs and feeding the hens. I could go for long walks with Michael sometimes and I wouldn't mind if he shot things.

It was pitch dark when we got back to Templegarve and Auntie Tess gave out to Michael, "Michael, for goodness sake, would you look at the time! The child must be wallfalling."

"Una's all right," Michael said, "aren't you Una?"

"Yes," I said, "I'm all right."

The next day I was out in the yard after dinner with a basin of scraps for the hens. I was standing there going "*Here* chuck chuck! Chuck chuck chuck!" and the hens were all coming skittering over to me, when I saw the first rat. He was in beside the wall of the barn, not moving, but his sides were going in and out as if he was tired, then he ran in behind the tractor and I didn't see him any more. I told Auntie Tess about seeing him and she said yes, there were a lot of rats around. She said they were taking eggs over beyond and Danny Molloy had to put down poison for them. I was glad we had the cats so they wouldn't take our eggs.

When I went over to Molloys, Brian showed me three dead rats. He said, "Come on down to the trough and we'll see them staggering along. It's great gas!"

"What is?"

"The rats. When they take the poison it goes to their brain and they get awful thirsty."

"Do they not die?"

"Of course they die, Stupid, but they go staggering around the place first, looking for water. You can easily get them with stones. Come on, would you!"

But I said "No, I want to go and talk to Bernie," and I went into the house and upstairs instead.

As soon as I went in the door Bernie said "Guess who gave me a lift home on Sunday night?"

I didn't know who.

"Mister Charming Brown Eyes," she said, but I still didn't know.

"Your cousin!" she said then, and I said "Oh, Michael?" I forgot that he went to dances on Sunday nights after I was in bed. He never said anything about them.

I told Bernie about the rats and asked her if it was true about the poison.

"Yes," she said, "it's cat when they're dying all over the place. I can't stand it, but you shouldn't have to use poison. They could billet them away."

"What do you mean, billet them?"

"It's a kind of a charm. It makes them go away somewhere else."

"How does it make them?"

"Rats got into our potato clamp up at home and my Granny wrote out a thing on a bit of paper. It's a message to the rats and when they see it they go away somewhere else."

"I don't believe that."

"I swear to God," she said. She licked her finger and made a cross on her throat. "I'm not telling you a word of a lie. You write it out on a bit of paper, 'Dear Rat, if you can read, keep away from my feed...' Something like that. When the king rat sees that he takes it in his mouth and he leads all the other rats out of there, over to the other side of the river, or someplace away."

On the way back home for my tea I saw another rat inside our gate, and I kept seeing rats after that, live ones and dead ones. We brought two of the cats into the house so the rats wouldn't come in there, and Auntie Tess said one night "You'll have to get some of that poison, Michael, they're too much for the cats."

I said, "Bernie knows something you can write down to make them go away."

"Oh Lord," Auntie Tess said, "what kind of nonsense has she been putting in the child's head?"

Michael winked at me, "What did Bernie say?" So I told them. Auntie Tess got up and began to clear the dishes and Teresa helped her, but Michael sat and listened. I said Bernie could probably get the exact words from her granny, but he looked at Auntie Tess and then he said, "That Bernie's a gas character, Una, but she's a bit thick, you know. You wouldn't want to mind the half of what she says."

The next day we were coming back from the creamery. We'd already got the newspaper and Michael stopped the car again. He came back and threw a packet onto the back seat.

"What is it?" I asked.

"Rat poison," he said. "We'll be fishing them out of the rain barrel, but it's better than having them in the feed."

"Is it really not true that Bernie's granny could charm them?"

"Not at all," he said. "That's only old pishogues," and he laughed. "Mind you though, when I was a little lad I heard somebody talking about seeing a whole crowd of rats coming along the road and the first one had a bit of paper in his mouth, going from one farm to another."

"Bernie said her granny did it a few years ago when there were rats in their potatoes."

He laughed again when I said that. He said "In Derrylynch, is it? Sure they're half-wild up there; you wouldn't know what they'd get up to. It's the back of beyond, that place." I didn't tell him that's what my Dad said about Templegarve.

I only had another week before I went back to school, and rats were beginning to die around our yard as well. I went to see Bernie one day. She said the dance was only fabulous on Sunday night, and started to tickle me. She looked at me in the mirror of her dressing table. She was putting on lipstick, sitting with just her slip on. "Did our friend Michael say anything about me?"

I didn't want to tell her he said she was a bit thick, so I said no. Then I went down into the yard.

Brian was there. He was walking across to the manure heap holding a dead rat by the tail.

"You won't see any of these fellas when you get back to Dublin," he said. I went around by the hayshed until I found another one and I picked it up by the tail too. I ran all the way to the manure heap with my hand over my mouth and threw it up there beside Brian's.

I didn't tell anyone about the rats when I got back to Dublin—I knew they'd think I was disgusting. I wrote a letter to Templegarve to say thank you for the lovely summer, and the lady next door told me I looked like a grand healthy country lassie.

I was back at school a good few weeks when a card came in a letter from Auntie Tess. I wasn't allowed to see the letter but the card was an invitation to the wedding of Miss Bernadette Garvey to Mr Michael Kenny. I thought my heart was broken for the first few minutes, but then I was just surprised, and excited at the idea of a wedding.

"Can we go?" I said, "Can I get a day off school?"

"No, no," my mother said. "It's too far."

"But they invited us."

"Eat your dinner," she said. "It's just a formality."

We did go to Templegarve the next summer, all of us—my mother, father, me, Eugene and the twins—just for the day. It looked the same, except maybe a bit smaller, and there was a long caravan up at the other end of the yard, and a clothesline beside it with about twenty nappies on it. The car wasn't there so I knew Michael was still at the creamery.

Auntie Tess said Bernie was feeding the baby but she'd bring him down after dinner, and she asked me if I wanted to take the twins out and show them the hens. Eugene came too and we saw Whitey with the one eye and some of the other cats. Whitey was dragging along so slowly I thought he probably only had about one life left. I told Eugene not to pet any of them, because they were wild. Then I saw the car coming into the yard with the trailer behind and I waved like mad. Michael waved back, but he didn't stop, just drove on up to the cowshed. I wanted to go up, but it was too muddy for the twins and I still had my good shoes on. I just stood and watched him unloading the milk churns.

When it was dinner time I said "I'll call Michael," but my mother came to the door after me and said "Come on, Una, Michael has to have his dinner in his own house."

"But that's not a house," I said. "That's only a caravan."

"That's enough," she said. "Now stop that. Come and eat your dinner."

She said it as though I'd done something really awful. I had a pain in my throat all through dinner from trying not to cry.

# NESTING

Are you sure you've had enough to eat? I know what that journey's like. Those last few miles are incredible. All that emptiness. Though actually the bog's interesting when you start looking at different plants and everything—Alastair could tell you all about them. I have to warn you though, he's so tired when he gets home these days you'll be lucky if he says hello.

It's amazing that you made it. I can't get over it. Remember the way everyone promised to come and see me? Well they all had great intentions till they looked at the map. You're the first one who's sat at that table. Is it like what you expected? Actually I can't stand the house. The landlord's a bit too fond of yellow. Come outside and look. The scenery's the good part.

I always come out here in the evening. I love the way the sun hits the mountains. All the little field walls stand out so clearly—that one's like lace against the sky, isn't it? And it's so still. There's even a corncrake in one of those fields. Do you know about corncrakes? They used to be all over the country, but they've got very rare. You only find them now in places like this, the west of Scotland, a few other places. The machinery's wiping them out and people are starting to get all nostalgic about them. You know the idea in the thirties, all the crossroads dances and couples courting behind haystacks? Then the priests built dancehalls so they could keep an eye on them, and it all stopped? Anyway it seems the corncrake was one bird they used always hear on summer nights. But it's the weirdest call, like something wooden. *Crake crake*. Like that. You'd hear it for miles. They come in from Africa to breed here. Alastair has loads of books about all that natural history stuff. I didn't know a thing about it when I got here, but it's a good way to pass the time.

There it is there—listen. Like bones scraping together. Listen. *Crake crake. Crake crake.* It's a mating call. He's somewhere down there in the hayfield. The males come first and stake out a territory, then they start up that racket, and females come and join them. He'll go on all night now, once he's started. He even kept me awake a couple of nights last week.

Of course it wasn't even dark. I love the long days really. It's nearly eleven now, see? And it's still daylight. Sometimes I'm just waiting for it to get dark so I can go to bed. It's ridiculous. Do you remember that poem?

> *In winter I get up at night*
> *And dress by yellow candlelight.*
> *In summer, quite the other way,*
> *I have to go to bed by day.*

Is it Robert Louis Stevenson? We learned it in the National School. It's not something you notice so much in the city, but my God you notice it here. Long days in summer, long nights in winter. I couldn't believe the winter. It wasn't daylight till nine and then it got dark again at four o'clock. I mean black dark. I felt I was getting smaller and smaller. I was crouching down under all the darkness. I still feel it a bit. I don't know if you notice—am I different from the way I used to be? It did something to me. I'd better not start though—Alastair's sick and tired of hearing me going on about it and he'll be back soon.

We could walk down as far as the road if you like. D'you see that there? That's a scarlet pimpernel. I never knew it was the name of a flower, did you? A lot of them grow among the carrots. And that's silverweed, with the yellow flower. See the silvery backing on the leaves? It's a bit hard to see in this light. They used to eat that during the Famine. The roots maybe. I'll have to dig one up sometime and see.

You still hear stories about the Famine here; there's ruins of houses all over the place. There must have been an awful lot more people living around here then. You can even see marks way up on the hillsides, really rough land where they used to have fields. I think that's why people here buy so many tins and packets. It drives Alastair crazy, but I think they remember too much about poverty.

Those are our vegetables. Carrots and leeks and beetroot and lettuce and then the spuds and cabbage and onions. That's dill down there—see the tall feathery stuff beside the elder tree? I'd no idea what it'd look like when I put the seeds in. Alastair kept laughing at me, but I was so sick of outside leaves of cabbage. Would you believe that's the only green thing we had all winter?

The one with the heads of white flowers, that's the elder. Alastair wants to make elderflower wine, but I can't work up much enthusiasm. It's supposed to be an unlucky tree. The wood's no good for anything except making whistles. They say it was used for the crucifixion and it's cursed ever since, so you're not even supposed to cut a stick from it to drive cattle.

You end up believing that sort of thing. "Elders and nettles and corncrakes: three signs of an abandoned house." There's an Irish saying for you: *trom, traonach is neantóg*. There are nettles in there too, see? They grow wherever people pissed. Wherever they emptied their chamberpots, I suppose. They like nitrogen.

That house over there—the two chimneys in the trees—the woman in that house just had twins. But wait till I tell you—she already had fourteen kids. She's a nice woman. I talk to her sometimes when I walk over that way. I think that was part of the problem. Alastair started here last May, but I didn't come till September and then it was really wet, so I didn't get to know any of the women before the winter set in. They hardly ever go out you know. You only meet them if you go to their houses, and the men don't really talk to strange women at all.

We're unusual too, that we're not related to anyone. Mary Dick's one though. I went to see her in hospital. And she has a sister, back the other way, that talks to me as well. Can you imagine though? Sixteen kids. The big ones are all gone, of course. They're in England and Boston and places. But imagine being pregnant that many times? I suppose a lot of people were. Bach had twenty-two kids, didn't he? But were they all by the same wife? I can't remember. Mary Dick's a lovely woman. A great sense of humour, but I'd have sworn she was way over fifty till I saw her pregnant. She has hardly any teeth. It's a great name, isn't it? Mary Dick. Her father was Dick. I thought first it was her husband. That'd be just too much. And he's the most inoffensive-looking little man.

I walk down this way a lot. If you go left at the bottom you come to a pier. It's good that you're with me—if I walk on my own I get the feeling people think I'm weird. It's okay if you're a visitor, you can go anywhere you like, but if you live here it's different. Married women are supposed to have things to do. They all work really hard here. But then they all have kids. It's funny, the way people talk, I feel I'm supposed to be up in the house all the time, getting pregnant. But you'd think the way to get pregnant was staying inside by yourself all day, washing clothes and cooking.

Maybe that's the idea. Maybe you're so glad to see him at the end of the day that you jump on him when he comes in and tear the clothes off him? That's not the effect it has on me though. It must be my spoilt city upbringing—I'm not tough enough. When I was on my own all day in the beginning I just used to turn into this tight little lump of misery. Poor old Alastair had a lot to put up with.

*Crake crake*. There he goes again. *Crake crake*. All the way from Africa. I can't imagine how they get here. I mean obviously they fly, but they're not like swallows. They're big. You never see them flying. As soon as they get here they flop down into the long grass and that's that. They just stay there.

*Crake crake*.

*Crake crake*. I did a terrible thing the other night. I was up there on my own in the house when he started up with his craking, letting the world know he was there. I couldn't see him, of course. You hardly ever see a corncrake, but he got on my nerves, with his God-given right to be so stupid out there, saying the same thing, over and over. I don't know what got into me. I came flying out the door down the path, straight into the hayfield over the wall—I never knew I could run that fast. He was in there in the long grass, craking away, and I went crashing and flailing in through it, just to make him show himself. God knows what I did to the grass. I hope no one saw me, but in the end he flew up right in front of me. He's a little brown lump, like a young hen, a pullet. You'd never think something that apologetic-looking could make so much noise. I'm relieved he's still there though—I was afraid I'd chased him away, and Alastair'd kill me. Don't say anything to him, will you?

It just seems so stupid. What happens is the birds come from Africa and make nests in the hayfield or the cornfield or whatever, but now instead of men coming with scythes late in the summer to cut whatever it is, they either cut early for silage, or they bring in these big heavy machines, and the birds haven't a chance. The nest and the eggs get crushed to bits. You'd see egg-yolk smeared all around, and baby birds dead. But the worst thing is sometimes the hen bird won't leave the nest. They cut right through her legs while she's sitting there. I've seen pictures of them. They're still alive, but their feet are chopped off.

It's just the thought of that. Imagine coming all the way from Africa and then hunkering down in a hayfield until they come to cut your feet off?

# MAJELLA'S QUILT

We learned sewing in primary school. Tacking and running first, then backstitching and hemming and run-and-fell seams and buttonholes, on little blue specimens that the nun cut out with pinking shears. They got all sweaty and creased because we usually had to rip them out a few times, but when they were finished the nun smoothed them out under her hand and stuck them into our copybooks with tape. She kept fifty-two Calvita cheese boxes for us in the big press beside the blackboard, and every girl had one, with a specimen, a needle, a thimble and a spool of red thread. We were only seven or eight when we started. Our stitches were big and awkward, and we had to use red so she could see what was wrong with them, but by the time we got to sixth class we were able to do tiny white stitches on white material and you couldn't see them at all.

In Secondary, everything was different. I got a new school uniform that was miles too long for me and we didn't do sewing any more. There was a room with a row of sewing machines, but our class did Latin instead of Domestic.

By the end of first year my gymslip fitted me, but all my own clothes were too small.

"I'll knit, but I will not sew," my mother said. We had no sewing machine and I wanted her to get one. She was scraping batter out of the mixing bowl, laughing at me.

"I'll sew then," I said. "I'll make my own clothes." I was raging mad, but she just thought it was funny. "We can go to Dolores," she said, "as soon as you get your holidays. Calm down. Majella's coming over this afternoon."

"I'm not going back to Dolores. She thinks I'm about seven. She hasn't a clue what people my age wear."

I hated Dolores ever since she made me take my clothes off right there in the shop and stand in my vest and pants to get measured. She always had her mouth full of pins. She used to pull me and poke me whenever she was making anything.

"I bet she'd just make some hicky old thing with puffed sleeves or something," I shouted at my mother. "You don't even care." I left my schoolbag right there on the floor and stomped upstairs where I could cry without her laughing at me. Other girls' mothers made clothes for them, or showed them how to use the machine and they made their own: straight shifts with no sleeves, out of only two yards of material.

My summer dresses from last year all had gathered skirts and short sleeves. I got them in parcels from America or else horrible Dolores made them, but now I was so tall all the hems had to be let down. The bottom of all the skirts was a brighter colour than the rest, the tops were too tight and the waists were all up around my ribs. I'd even rather wear my school uniform.

Downstairs, I heard my mother opening the front door to Majella, and then they were laughing in the sitting room. I liked Majella. When I was small I used to think I could run away from home and she'd hide me, but after a while I realised she wouldn't be able to: Colm was in the Guards and he'd probably have to report me. If it was any other friend with Mam I'd have thought they were laughing at me, but I knew Majella wouldn't. I got up and went to the bathroom to wash my face.

Mam heard me on the landing.

"Una," she called up, "come down and say hello to Majella."

She got up from her chair when I came in, but she didn't smile. "I'm going to make a cup of tea. You sit down and talk to Majella."

Majella had straight, shiny red hair and freckles. She was tiny—not even as tall as me—but she was my idea of elegant. She was younger than Mam and her clothes were just beautiful. She wore eye make-up, not just lipstick and powder like my mother, and she had no children. She was always nice to us.

"How's Una?" she said. She was from Derry so her accent was lovely as well.

"I'm fine," I said. Majella always made me smile.

"Your Mammy tells me you're getting interested in sewing."

I felt myself getting red, but Majella was winking and shushing her lips with her finger.

"She said you were thinking of learning."

"We haven't got a machine," I said.

"I have a machine though. You could come and learn on my machine, couldn't you?"

"I'd probably only break it or something."

"You would not break it. I'd show you how to use it. I used to make all my own clothes, you know."

My mother came in with the tray. She seemed to have forgiven me. "That's right, Una. Do you not remember the lovely curtains too? Majella made them herself as well."

"The red ones in your sitting room? They're beautiful."

"The thing I can't do is knit," Majella said. She sat back in her chair. She looked at my mother and they both laughed.

"Don't you worry about the knitting," Mam said. "I'll get started on the bits of knitting." She put out cups and saucers. "I made a bit of toast for you, Majella. It's good to keep nibbling. Don't put butter on it unless you feel like it."

"I *hate* toast without butter," I said, and they both laughed again, but in a nice way. There was cake as well, still warm, but Majella didn't have any.

"I'm sorry, Mary. It looks gorgeous."

"Don't you worry," my mother said. "You'll have plenty of time to eat cake."

"So come round to me, Una," Majella said when she was leaving. "Come round on Saturday afternoon, if you like."


Everything in our house was tall, and a bit narrow, but Majella's and Colm's house was modern. Everything was low and flat. There was one big room all the way from the front to the back and a long wide window at each end, with dark red velvet curtains. "Are those the curtains you made yourself?" I asked her.

"They are indeed," she smiled at me. "I'm not supposed to lift anything, Una. Maybe you could get the machine out."

I put the machine on the dining-room table, on top of an old blanket, and Majella showed me how to guide the thread in and out of all the different places and then through the eye of the needle from behind, and how to wind the bobbin and adjust the tension. She had a whole spool of thread left over from the red curtains and we did lines and zigzags all over a bit of an old white sheet. She showed me how to go backwards along my own stitches to finish off.

"A cup of tea," she said. I unplugged the machine and wound the flex round the foot pedal the way she showed me, and put it back under the stairs.

"Will I tell you a secret?" We were sitting in the kitchen. "I'm going to have a baby."

I couldn't get my breath for a minute, "Does Mam know?"

"Oh yes." Majella gave me a huge smile. "I just have to be a bit careful." She stopped smiling, "I lost the last one."

I was confused, but then she said "I don't mean I had a baby and then I lost it. I had a miscarriage. You know what that is, don't you?"

"Sort of." Majella always treated me like a grown-up, so I was embarrassed that I didn't really.

"You know the way you get your period every month?"

I was really red now. My first period was only a few weeks before that. I could still feel the shock of the red on my knickers.

"Well, when you're expecting a baby you don't have any periods. That's how you know at the beginning. But if something goes wrong you start to bleed a bit, and sometimes you lose the baby. So the doctor wants me to be very careful."

I took a deep breath. "Is it just like a period then?"

"Well, it's a lot more blood. It's not very nice."

"It must be awful." I didn't want to think about it.

"It is," Majella said. "It's awful when it happens, but it's not going to happen this time, so you're not to worry." She smiled at me again. "Anyway, I'm supposed to take it easy, so if you'd like to bring some material around, I'll help you to make a dress. You'd be company for me."

"Are you sure?" I said. My face was still hot, but it wasn't burning any more.

"Of course I'm sure! You get some material and a spool of thread and bring them here to me. I have plenty of patterns. We'll make a dress for you in no time. You can do all the work—I'll keep my feet up!"

I had my own money saved from selling lines, so after school on Monday I got the bus into town in my uniform and went to buy material. I knew exactly where to go. I got two yards of blue cotton with little rows of pink rosebuds on it, and a spool of blue thread.

Majella thought the material was lovely. We went through all her patterns till we found a straight shift, and she said her size would fit me even though I was taller.

"You're about the same size as me on top. Or the size I was before all this started." She patted her stomach and winked at me. I smiled back. I didn't even mind when she took out her tape and measured me around the chest.

I couldn't believe how easy it was. I thought a pattern for a dress would be like a knitting pattern, all little numbers and complicated instructions, but it was big pieces of tissue paper. We spread the material out on her dining-room table and folded it in two. Then we laid the paper onto it and Majella showed me how to put in two pins in opposite directions to mark the places where the darts should be. We pinned all around the edges and cut around the black lines, and by the time Colm came home the first evening we had my dress all ready to start sewing. It was full of pins, so I left it there when I went home, but I brought a scrap of the material with me.

I did all the sewing myself, except for putting in the zip. I'd forgotten to buy one, but Majella said I could have one that was in her work-basket. She even showed me an easy way of doing it—sewing the join up as though it was a seam, only with a long stitch you could rip out later. Then I did the hem by hand.

We were sitting at the fire in Majella's living room, about two weeks after the first time I went. I'd put away the machine, filled the coal bucket and washed my hands, and I was sitting doing the hem. Majella was on the couch with her feet up, looking at a big library book.

She said to me, "Do you like sewing, Una?"

"Yes I do. At least, I think I will when I really learn how."

"No," she said, "I mean hand sewing. Do you like it?"

"I suppose so, if it's nice material."

"Wait till I show you something. Will you give me the bag that's down beside your chair?"

The bag was full of bits of material, gorgeous velvet in all different colours: red from the curtains, but black and blue as well, and green, and some pieces of very pale pink. I brought it over to her.

"This pink was a cloak I wore when we got married," she said. "Eight years ago. Imagine. It was Stephen's Day so I had to have something warm."

Eight years ago I was only five.

"I was thinking of making a patchwork quilt out of all this. Come here till you see." She opened the book again and showed it to me. Nearly every second page was a photograph.

"It's from America. They do a lot of it over there."

I was turning the pages and every picture was of a quilt. All different colours and patterns.

"Show me a minute," Majella took the book from me. "There's a kind called a crazy quilt that they used to make out of velvet." She turned the pages till she found it, "Look at that there, Una. Tell me, did you ever see anything like that?"

It was like a picture of jewels—bright shining colours all joined together in different shapes.

"And look here. See the way it's all embroidered in between the pieces? It's the same red silk thread all the way through. Look, little flowers in some of the corners."

"That looks like a name," I said.

"It is a name. The woman that made it. *Eliza Cady, 1888*. Wouldn't that be a lovely thing to leave after you?"

"I think I like the one on the other page better," I said, "the one that looks like geese flying."

Majella didn't even hear me. She was looking at another picture and she didn't say anything for ages.

"I started to make one once before, a bit like this."

"Did you not finish it?"

"No." Her voice sounded very tired, "I think it got thrown out. It was a baby quilt, when I was pregnant before. Little squares of cotton like your dress. All different blues." She gave a strange laugh, "I don't know what I'd've done if it was a girl."

That was on a Monday, and I didn't go over on Tuesday. When I got home from school on Wednesday Mam told me Majella was in hospital.

"I don't know," she said. "It doesn't look too good."

She went in to see Majella that evening and I watched television with Dad and Eugene. When Mam came home she said Majella was holding on but she wasn't allowed to put a foot to the ground.

"She'd love to see you though, Una, if you had time to visit her."

Mam took her coat off and gave it to me to hang up, "She's in a ward with five other women, and one of them never stops crying, God love her. You could go in after school, couldn't you Una? She hasn't any visitors in the afternoon with Colm working all day. She's doing needlework though. Hand sewing. She'd love to show it to you."

I remembered the hospital smell from visiting my Granny before she died, so I felt funny walking along the corridor. I was looking for St Anne's ward, but there was a woman in a pink dressing-gown walking slowly in front of me, with her hand on her side. I didn't want to go marching on past her, but I didn't want her to think I was following her either, so I kept stopping. I saw women sitting up in beds, reading magazines and putting on nail varnish, and a woman trying to get out of a bed, holding onto the mattress with her two hands and feeling on the floor with her foot for her slippers. I saw a couple of women with huge stomachs. It was a maternity hospital, but I didn't see any babies.

When I found St Anne's I couldn't see Majella. There were six beds, with browny-pink curtains around them, and the one nearest the door was empty. All the others had so many flowers around them you could hardly see the people.

Then I saw her, sitting up with about five pillows behind her. Another woman in a dressing-gown was sitting on her bed, but when I came she patted Majella's hand and said "Here's your friend now, I'll leave you," and I got a chair from near the window. The other woman walked away slowly and I sat down. At the door she turned and smiled back at us.

"She's nice," I said, and Majella said "She's great, that woman. Carmel her name is." Her voice was very quiet and her eyes were red. "She goes around cheering everyone up. She has six children at home and she's after having her womb removed now. Would you believe she's only forty?"

"She looks much older." My mother was forty-one, but this woman had grey hair.

"That's what a hard life does to you. The stories she told me about the doctors down the country! But tell me, did you finish your hem?"

I told her about the dress. I had it finished but I'd only had a chance to try it on once, because of school.

Majella smiled, "I'll tell you what you'll do. When are you getting your holidays?"

"Tomorrow. We have a half day."

"Would you come in and see me for a little while in the afternoon? Would you? And model your new dress for me?"

I was delighted. "Yeah. Do you really want me to? I could, I suppose."

I asked her what it was like in the hospital.

"It's all right. It's hard to sleep. Then they wake you up at all hours of the morning. But at least that girl beside the door is gone."

"What was wrong with her?"

"She never shut up. All day long and all night, crying. She lost her baby. The others were all real nice to her. I was sorry for her, you know, but I just couldn't listen to her. The sound of that crying went through me."

I remembered the other thing my mother said.

"Mam said you were doing needlework."

"That's right. Do you want to see it?" She pulled out some velvet from under a magazine on the bed, "I started my crazy quilt."

She'd joined two pieces of red to a piece of black. They were rough, jagged shapes though, and different sizes.

"Do you not use squares?"

"That's what they were all asking me here. This is a crazy quilt. Do you not remember it in the book? It means any old shape that's not a square. The girls here think I'm the crazy one—they think red and black are awful together, but that's the colours I want to use. I'm making a whole lot of pieces like this. I'll put in other colours later, when I join them all up. It's not a baby quilt, you know. You couldn't give velvet to a baby. She can have it when she's grown-up."

"Do you think it's going to be a girl?"

"I think it is. I think it's a girl."

I wore my new dress the next day to show Majella, and she made me take off my cardigan and turn around to show Carmel. But when Carmel went back to the other ward I saw Majella's eyes were all red, and then she started to cry, lying back on the pillow with her face open.

"I'm bleeding again," she said, sniffling. She reached out for my hand. I gave her a tissue out of her box with the other hand. "It was all on the sheets this morning. I'm sorry Una, I just can't stop crying. Colm won't be in till tonight." She sopped at her face with the tissue. It was as though something had burst inside her head, the way she cried.

"Do you know what Carmel told me? She was in terrible form herself today. She said one of the nurses said you wouldn't sew up an animal the way they did her after the last baby."

Majella's shoulders were going up and down and her nose was running. I was getting frightened but none of the other women took any notice and there was no nurse. I gave Majella some more tissues, and poured her a glass of water. I put my arm around her shoulders. I didn't know what to do, but she was talking again.

"That old doctor doesn't even look at you when he talks to you." She started to cry again, "Carmel showed me the stitches he put in her for the hysterectomy." Her voice was gulping.

"Ssh," I said.

"It was like bootlaces, Una; great big black buckstitches all the way up her stomach!"

She sounded as though she was choking. I held onto her shoulders and she cried some more. Then she blew her nose and said "I think I'll lie down."

"There's a woman doctor here now," she said in a faint voice when I thought she was asleep. "Doctor Coffey. I'm going to see if I can change over to her."

I didn't know what I should say. Majella's eyes were closed but she was still talking, nearly whispering. "Anne over at the window said she's great. She said you'd want to see the lovely neat little stitches she puts in women. I should try to get her, shouldn't I?" Majella was trying to smile. Her eyes were open again.

I tried to smile as well, "I don't know. Maybe."

"Your roses are lovely," I said after a while, but Majella was asleep. The bit of quilt she showed me yesterday was sticking out of her locker, red and black. I pulled it out to look at it. Two triangles, a big black one and a little red one, and a red piece with four sides, a quadrangle. All the stitching was black, tiny and neat. I put it back and whispered to Majella, "I'm going now," but she didn't wake up.

I didn't start to cry myself until I got out in the grounds of the hospital, and then I couldn't stop. I only had one tissue—a pink one from Majella's box that I didn't even know was in my hand. I sat down on the wall beside the gate so that I wouldn't have to get on the bus crying, and I stared at a place on the ground until I could breathe properly again. I kept seeing white sheets with red on them, and Carmel's stomach, laced like a boot, but I tried to concentrate on the crazy quilt in Majella's book, with its pink patches and blue patches and green patches, holding the angry red and black safely between them, and then the beautiful neat embroidery of red silk stitches joining them all together.

# OHIO BY THE OCEAN

In Ohio, Finn and Eithne sleep on a mattress on the floor in Finn's big room. Three of the walls have windows. One is filled with slender leaves now, from the big weeping willow in the yard, but the room still has more light than anywhere Eithne has ever slept.

The mattress is queen size. She thought at first it was an affectation, like a water-bed, or a mirror on the ceiling, but by June when the temperature stayed in the nineties for days on end, she saw the point.

Now it's August, and hot again. Still she needs a sheet over her at night, but Finn is lying sprawled on top of it.

Eithne tugs, trying to release it.

"I can't lie under the sheet if you're on top of it. It's like a strait-jacket."

"Lie on top," he mutters softly, his mouth drooling open, "Hot."

When sleep comes over Finn it fells him like a tree. Night after night Eithne finds herself enchanted and exasperated, contemplating the careless brown length of him.

"I can't lie on top. I'm too exposed. An eagle could swoop down and take me."

"No eagles." Finn grunts and heaves, mutters, and the sheet is free. He curls sweetly into his rapid eye movement position and Eithne lies on her back, the sheet up to her chin, looking at the stars through the farthest window.

It has no curtain. None of the windows had, when she arrived, but she bought a dark blue Indian bedspread for the big one on the right that faces the street. It hangs gracefully from two nails, and falls in a puddle of darkness on the floor.

There aren't any eagles in Ohio, it's true, but there are mosquitoes. Once as she slept, one bit her bare shoulder, and the swelling and itching stayed for weeks. Next morning they found a hole in the window screen, but Finn said he could mend it. They went to the hardware store and he bought a little repair kit, especially for screens.

"We have to take care of you," he said. "I've never seen anyone swell up like that from a mosquito bite."

"Well there aren't any in Ireland."

"No mosquitoes?"

"None I've ever seen." Eithne looked anxiously around at the shelves and racks. Irish skin is made for cool cloudy weather: thin and pink; it burns easily. Mosquitoes love it.

An electric fan stood whirring in one corner on the rough wooden floor, nodding from side to side on its pedestal, cooling the air. Two heavy-set men in overalls, tee-shirts and baseball caps stood calmly, waiting for service at the paint counter.

"It's probably not warm enough."

"And no snakes?"

"No snakes. Saint Patrick got rid of them."

"That's what my Dad used to say." He grinned at her. "No snakes in Ireland. God's own country," he went on piously, "the island of snakes and scholars."

"Saints and scholars."

"Saints, right."

Too late she saw it was a joke. Snakes and scholars. Not bad. Finn liked it when she laughed at his jokes, though it didn't bother him if she didn't. He was poking among the tools now, breathing in the leathery metallic smell, delighted with this treasure house of things to play with.

"Hey, look at this. Socket wrenches! A full set for twelve dollars. I don't have any socket wrenches."

"This is what I like." Eithne was looking at a rack of tool-belts. "Maybe I'll get one of these for my brother." Since meeting Finn's sisters she's been trying to tell him about her family, find details that will mean something to him.

"You know, Rónán? He's always up on ladders fixing gutters and things. It's a really American thing, I think." She held up the tool-belt. It had pockets for screwdrivers and chisels, loops for pliers and a hammer. "Like holsters for guns, you know, six-shooters? It was one of the first things I noticed when I came here. All these guys with their tools hanging down below their hips...." She laughed and looked around guiltily. No one had heard. The men in baseball caps were deep in talk. The fan still whirred mindlessly, near and then far, and in the troughs of silence between the waves, their voices came clearly.

"Way I look at it," the younger one was saying, "It don't matter a whole lot what religion y'are."

"Long as y'accept Jesus Christ as y'r personal saviour," the older one agreed, "it don't matter one bit."

"How about poison ivy?" Finn had come up behind her.

"No poison ivy either."

"Hey!" he whirled her around among the work gloves and the garden hoses, "That St Patrick was a pretty neat guy. Why don't we go there?"

"Ireland? I am going, probably." Eithne's voice was flat. She put the tool-belt back.

In bed remembering, she feels the flatness again. Her leave of absence ends in another three weeks. If she's not staying, she must go back, but Finn won't talk about it. He says it's her decision.


Ohio outside the windows is flat. Flat and full of trees. Their yard and the neighbours' yards, not even fenced: lawns and trees and houses and quiet streets.

Beyond the edge of town, roads run dead straight, five miles apart, and meet at right angles between cornfields. Last week their journey began with a road that ran straight westward between the papery golden rows of corn, but all summer Eithne has been riding her heavy blue bike on expeditions that were perfect rectangles, past storybook wooden houses with wraparound porches elaborately carved and spindled, great white wooden barns looming over them like cathedrals. Their roof-tiles spelled out names and dates: *Hofstetter 1866; Braun 1892*. All around were distance and warm silence. The big pale sky and faded land shimmered, dry while she sweated, like soft hardworking cotton clothes washed and washed again and spread in strong sunlight to dry.

Mountains and the ocean are what she pines for. Mountains and the sea she'd say at home, but here they say the ocean. It's so far to either coast; so hard to find a place that's higher than any other place, somewhere she could look out and down.

But Finn's sisters went to Ireland and what they missed there was trees and flat space—and Häagen Dazs ice-cream. Butter pecan. They drove around in a white rented car and visited their father's relatives in Leitrim.

Eithne tries to imagine them in Ireland. Strong golden skin like Finn's, white American smiles and denim jackets—Hi, I'm Colleen Maguire and this is my sister Erin? Expecting to be liked, as though that was their birthright. But apparently they were liked. Well why wouldn't they be? And nobody fell down laughing at their names. They were nineteen and twenty-one. They worked two jobs each for a year to save money for their trip. They just knew it would be wonderful, so of course it was.

Last week she and Finn took a special trip to the Twin Cities, to meet them and see where he grew up. While he's asleep she's trying to read back all that happened.

They shared the driving through cornfields and orchards and the edges of city after city on six-lane highways, through Wisconsin, to Minnesota. She felt like an American. Then in St Paul, car dealerships and dry cleaners had names she recognised—O'Sullivan, Ahearne. Finn told her about Archbishop Ireland in the nineteenth century, who persuaded Irish Catholics to venture westwards into this hilly place among the flat lakes and forests of the Protestant

Scandinavians, and suddenly she was Irish again, following her own people.

But when she met the Maguires their warmth overwhelmed her. She could only curl back into herself, surly in a corner. She refused to believe they could be real.

"Tha ocean," Colleen and Erin said, not "thee ocean." They saw it for the first time when they went to Ireland. Finn says "thee ocean," but he's a history teacher. Colleen dropped out of community college after one year. Now she waits tables in the fanciest restaurant in Minneapolis, and Erin goes to beauty school. "A accident," Erin said, "I saw a accident."

The pictures of their trip were so strange—like trick photographs taken at a fun-fair. Irish families posed awkwardly outside windswept bungalows, like anyone's relatives, but there stuck in among them were the two smiling candyfloss heads. None of them seemed to notice Eithne's own dark hair lying flat against her head, or that she wore no make-up, and hardly smiled. The napkins they used for dinner had shamrocks embroidered on them. Along with their roast beef they ate fruit salad with marshmallows in it.

Leona, their mother, is Ukrainian. But that means American, with ancestors who came from the Ukraine.

"I've never been to Ireland," she told Eithne. "I like the heat. And now I feel too old. Michael always wanted to go." She nodded towards the photo on the wall. "He loved everything Irish. Funny, he never got to go there."

As they left, Finn hugged his mother and his two sisters. Long sleepy hugs—whole conversations could take place inside them. Eithne stood by and waited. She and Finn were staying across the river in Minneapolis—she'd have to wait her turn until they got there. But Leona hugged her too, and when Erin and Colleen said goodnight they did as well.

"They really liked you," Finn said later, his lips against her breast, deep in the night in his friends' air-conditioned apartment.

"I liked them," she said doubtfully, "I never saw a family get on so well."

"Yeah," he said, nuzzling lower, impatient to stop talking. "We all really love each other."

Eithne plays that back in her mind now, lying beside Finn in the blue darkness of Ohio, listening for any note of sarcasm. She can find none. Finn really loves his family, and they really love him, and each other. They really loved his father too, Michael Maguire, the Irishman who'd never been to Ireland. He hung the Irish flag above the porch every St Patrick's day, and he called his firstborn only son, for God's sake, Finn McCool.

They took two days to drive home. And this evening Finn drove her to Lake Erie forty miles away, to see a beach.

"It's almost like the ocean," he said. Thee ocean. "The Great Lakes are as big as plenty of seas."

It was cool by the lake, and there were boats, but the beach was tiny—more like an overworked playground at home, with people making the best of things. The air was limp and lifeless without salt; even the setting sun looked dull.

They bought hamburgers in McDonald's somewhere up by the Lake and headed south again between the cornfields.

Finn drove in silence and Eithne watched the sky's faded calico change to dark blue silk. Far to their right it still carried a flush of pink, and the corn stood tall and secretive, holding its feathery tassels high and dark against it.

"You know I've decided I really like the corn," she said at last. Finn didn't turn his head, but she saw his face relax.

"It's so dignified. I love the way it grows to that height in just one season." She touched his arm, "Would there be mosquitoes if I opened the window?"

Finn turned and smiled at her, "Not while we're moving."

Eithne rolled down her window and lay back in the seat as the warm breeze covered her. Great crowding shapes of trees blotted out the pinkness of the west, and in the unexpected dark Finn's voice said "Skunk."

What? A sudden smell distracted her from what he'd said. She couldn't breathe deeply enough, trying to catch the vivid pungency that drifted through the car and out again.

"What was it? Was that a skunk?" Thinking comic-talk: You dirty, no-good skunk! That skunk! "I thought they smelt awful."

"They do, if you get close enough. I kinda like them."

"Why did we smell it?"

"Musta been a road kill."

"It's wonderful. It's like nothing I ever imagined."

Now while Finn sleeps, Eithne tries to recall the exhilaration of that smell. It was in her memory tonight as they made love: wild and warm, far from fruit salad with marshmallows, and napkins embroidered with shamrocks.

She remembers her own mother walking across the Bog of Allen in Kildare, laughing, throwing her head back and breathing deeply, "It's like the sea, Eithne, isn't it? The bog is like the sea, with all that air."

I see what you mean, Mom, she thinks, smiling wryly in the dark. The corn is like the sea too, and so are dead skunks on the road at night.

# MAYONNAISE TO THE HILLS

"Knock, knock."

"Who's there?"

"Mayonnaise."

"Mayonnaise who?"

"Mayonnaise have seen the glory of the coming of the Lord."

"Oh God!" Lucy laughed. Slowly her elbow shifted across the table.

"Sorry." Eithne emerged from behind the open fridge door, brandishing the jar. "Tuna's a bit depressing without something to lubricate it."

"I just can't bear to shop. I don't know what to buy any more."

"Well, just buy the things you can buy. It'll come back." Eithne stood for a moment with the tin-opener in her hand, looking at her. Lucy's shoulders were curved like an old woman's, bony in her thin sweater.

Eithne scraped the tuna into a bowl and paused with mayonnaise swelling on her knife blade, "Tuna's okay anyway. It's good for you." The mayonnaise dolloped into the bowl and she used the knife to mix it in. "I found a really easy recipe for a pasta sauce with tuna." The bread was white sliced pan. Eithne put four slices in the toaster. "You fry an onion and some garlic in olive oil, then chop up a tin of anchovies — do you like anchovies?"

Lucy nodded, smiling slightly.

"Well you chop up the anchovies and add them in and cook them. They sort of dissolve. Then you put in some olives and a tin of tuna, all broken up. It's wonderful," she licked her lips and grinned, "salty and oily and sort of smoky. You use lots of olive oil."

The toast popped up. Lucy's head was still nodding, but her shoulders shook and tears splashed onto the table. Eithne sat down and waited. "I know." She laid her hand on Lucy's arm. "It's awful. I'm just so sorry I couldn't be here for the funeral."

"You rang," Lucy sniffed long and wetly, "and you wrote." She reached for the box of tissues.

"I know. But I wanted to be here."

"Yeah," Lucy's red, wet, thin face smiled. "But I did feel you were here. I knew you would have been, if you could. In a way it's better that you're home now. I think I've been saving you up."

"How's that?"

"Well everyone was fantastic to me. But you know even with the best will in the world, people only give you about six months."

"I suppose."

"They've got used to the shock themselves. They've managed to process the fact that he's dead. But I still walk into the room with my mouth open to say something to him."

Eithne squeezed Lucy's arm and stood up. She poured glasses of milk. Spread the tuna on two slices of toast. Laid the other slices on top. Cut the sandwiches in four. Children's food. Lucy was still talking. About the agony of small things. Dealing with the hospital, the relatives, the colleagues, the funeral. She managed. Got through. But something simple like opening the door to the garage defeated her completely. Reduced her to sobbing and shaking.

"I have these awful dreams. One of them—I'm not even sure it was a dream. I woke up convinced I was remembering it. I was walking downtown somewhere, taking all my clothes off. I think I was looking for Frank. I was standing at the corner of a street, waiting to cross at the lights, with my tee-shirt in my hand and no bra on." She looked pleadingly at Eithne.

"I'd say if you'd really done that, there'd have been repercussions," Eithne smiled. "I think you're safe enough."

"I hope so. But you know in the dream one of the worst things was that nobody seemed to notice anything strange."

Eithne shook her head. "It's a dream. It's your mind dealing with it."

"And then for months after it happened, when I had my period I'd go to the bathroom to change my tampon. I'd take out the old one, but I'd forget to put the new one in. So I kept on finding myself bleeding and bleeding."

"Oh God! Oh Lucy!"

"The last few months it's been better. But once I was in town. I had to go straight into the first pub and it was this awful squalid smelly place. No seats on the loos, no towels, no toilet paper. The people looked as though they'd never seen daylight. I got raging mad with Frank for dying: if you hadn't died I wouldn't be here in this place, sort of thing. And I was dressed for work—skirt, tights, the lot." Her head came up and Eithne saw something like energy in her face. "The most grotesque things happen to you. But that helps in a way. You get a few laughs. It helps you see things differently."

"It's great if you can laugh."

Lucy nodded, grinning tentatively, "I keep throwing snails in next door. I'm afraid they'll complain."

"Why?"

"I'm afraid I'll hit someone, or they'll notice they have too many snails."

"Why do you throw snails?"

"They're all on the clematis. Dozens of them. They live there. Every time it rains I see them munching along, chewing up the leaves. And then in dry weather I go out and I can see them asleep, curled up behind the trellis. They're huge. Sometimes it's all I do. I look out the window and cry. Then I get some energy and I go out and throw snails over the wall."

"Eat your sandwich," Eithne said gently.

"What? Oh." Lucy began to eat.

Eithne opened the back door and walked over to the trellis. Found a snail, round, fat and dry, and flung it over the wall. "I see what you mean," she called through the open door. "It's quite satisfying."

Lucy came to the door. God she was thin.

"Maybe you should get away for a few days, Lucy. What do you think?"

"I don't know. It'd do me good, I suppose."

"I have to go to Kerry next week. Did I tell you my sister bought a place? You know, Gráinne? She wants me to go down and look at it. I have to talk to a builder for her, but she says it's quite habitable. You could come with me; it wouldn't be like a hotel or a B & B. You could do what you liked. I'd have to leave you alone a good bit, but I'd be around."

Lucy looked up, seemed interested.

"Or you could come on the train, so I'd have the house warmed up and aired before you got there."

Upstairs in Eithne's sister's house, thirty-five yards from the Atlantic, Lucy stands at a window, looking through salt-fogged glass at the blur of green and grey landscape outside. Eithne met her at the train, gave her a long warm hug and drove her here, but now she's alone. Eithne stayed long enough to give her tea, and banana bread with butter; then she went out somewhere in the rain. To see a man about a dog, she said. The old brown horse is still standing by the fence. His head is up. Eithne had a theory about him.

"When I got here on Sunday he looked quite healthy. He was standing beside the fence eating grass. But then on Monday the weather was filthy and he didn't move all day—just stood in the same place with his head hanging down. Yesterday it was a bit better—sunny intervals, so the head came up some of the time. He's still in the same place today, but I reckon you can tell by the head whether it's safe to go out."

The horse takes a weary step forward as Lucy watches. It bends its head and munches some grass. "Good on you, boy," she says, amused.

The room has pink distemper walls, a rangy, sagging bed, bare pale dusty floorboards where Lucy's paisley-patterned bag sits incongruously, and a hook on the back of the door. In the corners of the window-sill are nests of dust. A dry grey secretive quiet in the whorls of spiders' webs. Male spiders make one kind of web. Females make another. But which made this dense, deep, spiral kind? All Lucy's body-openings have felt like that for months: silent and dry like those webs.

In the kitchen downstairs, the walls are painted dark green gloss below, knicker-pink above. A Sacred Heart picture hangs on the wall; a long-haired Christ pointing reproachfully at his damaged heart. His little red lamp is unlit, but there's a fire of turf and the room is dry and warm. Lucy wipes crumbs off the oilcloth that covers the table, and washes the tea mugs. Potatoes, carrots and parsnips sit, washed and scraped, in bowls of water on the draining board.

Eithne comes in. "It wasn't a dog," she says, shaking raindrops out of her hair.

"What wasn't?"

"I said I had to see a man about a dog. But it wasn't a dog, it was a fish!" Triumphantly she lifts the pocket-flap of her oilskin jacket. A glimmering tail curves up out of it. Carefully she produces the fish, "It's completely illegal—and it's very, very fresh." Her wet face glistens as she grins. "They're using monofilament nets that the salmon can't see, but this one's already caught so I have no moral qualms about eating it."

"How did you know?"

"Gráinne's builder tipped me off that if I could sort of wander past the pier at about five o'clock, I might discover something to my advantage. Let's put the spuds on."

"What'll you do with the carrots and parsnips?"

"I was going to just steam them till they're soft and then mash them up with butter and black pepper. And we can grill the fish. Keep it simple."

Lucy catches up with Eithne on the bridge after they've eaten. First she said she'd just stay in the house—she's eaten more than she has in months and they've drunk a whole bottle of wine; Eithne can walk faster and further without her. But here she is, wearing two pairs of socks inside Gráinne's wellingtons, splashing through the bright puddles on the shiny black road.

"I think I really have a sexual relationship with mountains," Eithne is saying as she reaches her.

Lucy laughs gently through her nose. The evening is luminous after a day of rain. "You what?"

"No, I'm serious. I really get turned on. You have no idea how miserable I was in Ohio. The flatness of it nearly killed me."

"I didn't know you were miserable."

"Well, not miserable. There were all sorts of things I liked a lot. But I felt a bit like Heidi when she went to boarding school. Did you read that one? Where she kept hiding her white bread to bring back to Peter and the Alm Uncle and it all went mouldy? I was pining for my Alm a bit."

Lucy leans on the rail beside her. The mountain is bald and elegant against the sky, reflecting the sunset from its many slopes, and the river runs down it towards them, swollen, brown and frilly between green banks. "Anybody would."

"Come on, let's walk. The road doubles back up here and we'll see a lot more. You know, just the other day I saw this illustration in a book I picked up. A line drawing, in a book of poetry. I don't know what the hell it had to do with the poems, except that they were by a man, but it showed all these rolling hills against the horizon. Then you said to yourself, Hold on! What are those clumps of trees doing there and there and there?"

Lucy looks back when Eithne stops talking and sees her looking, waiting for her to understand.

"Clumps of trees? Oh."

"Yes. Hills are breasts, and the earth is a woman, and a woman is the earth and all that crap."

"It's a bit pathetic though, isn't it?"

"Well, it is. But what I'm trying to say is I think landscape turns anyone on. Or it can—but men think sex belongs to them."

"Hmm."

"I suppose it's because of the age I was when we came here first. We came for our holidays when I was thirteen and fourteen and fifteen and I'm sort of imprinted. But the thing is, it's me *with* the land, not me *as* the land."

Lucy laughs. "I always thought the landscape thing was a big fat, old-fashioned woman anyway. Lush, fertile land — ploughing and all that — voluptuous. This all seems a bit bony to me."

"But that's just what I'm saying! Plenty of women are thin—just look at you. And plenty of men are fat. It doesn't matter whether it's a man or a woman; the land can just do it to you. I once had an orgasm just sitting on a rock up here."

Lucy looks at her. Eithne turns pink, "I never told anyone that before." She laughs, "Are you shocked? I just feel so alive when I come down here. I walk along the road and smell the turf smoke and the salty air and I want to open my mouth and my nose wider and wider to take it in. And then at night the sky is so clean. You feel if you could open wide enough you could swallow the stars. That's what sex is about after all, isn't it? Feeling everything waking up?"

"Mm. I suppose it is, a bit."

"Oh Lucy, I'm sorry."

"No, it's okay."

Eithne looks carefully and sees that it is. Lucy's eyes are still looking out, animated, not stunned by some invisible horror, hidden behind her face the way they were in Dublin.

"I was looking at spiders' webs up in the house today," she says slowly. "I was thinking that's what I'm feeling like now: dry and fragile, you know? But I think I like your idea better." She smiles. "An orgasm sitting on a rock, eh?"

"Mm-hm," Eithne nods solemnly, her eyes bright and wicked, "Mind you, it was a good bit warmer."

They reach the top of the hill. Over on their left the bay sparkles. Little pink clouds line up busily behind the nearest headland and the breeze blowing up the slope is dry. Still laughing, they turn back down to the house.

"I think I'll walk on up this way, if you don't mind," Lucy says when they get to the bridge. "I haven't had nearly as much exercise as you have today."

"Fine." Eithne hugs her with one arm. "Take your time. I have to write a letter anyway. Go and talk to the mountain."

Wellingtons are not the best for walking, but with two pairs of socks they're not bad. Lucy stops halfway up the headland path to pull her socks up. She straightens and waves to Eithne, unlocking the house door down below. The taste of salmon and white wine lingers in her mouth.

Across the valley, in front of her as she walks, the setting sun laps against the mountainside, golden and alive. Frank would have loved it. Probably. She's loving it anyway, all by herself, she realises. Actually Frank would have looked at it, but he probably would have stayed in the car, with his book.

She sees herself, huddled and slumped at the kitchen table in Dublin, month after month, and takes a breath, feeling the wind come gently through the open zip front of her jacket, sifting through the woollen stitches of her sweater, touching the skin on the insides of her breasts. The light on the side of the mountain has already changed.

"I will lift up mine eyes to the hills." Lucy takes a little, sharp breath. "I will lift up mayonnaise...." She knuckles deeper into the corners of her pockets and walks taller.

❦ 278 ❦